ONLY IN DREAMS

THE STUBBORN LOVE SERIES

WENDY OWENS

ORANGEWILLOW PUBLISHING

Only In Dreams

Copyright © 2014 by Wendy Owens

Editing services provided by Madison Seidler of MadisonSeidler.com

Proofreading provided by Chelsea Kuhel of

Cover by WENDY OWENS

Without limiting the rights under copyright reserved above, no part of this publication may be reproduced, copied or transmitted, in any form without the prior written permission of the author of this book.

This book is a pure work of fiction. The names, characters, or any other content within is a product of the author's imagination. The author acknowledges the use of actual bands and restaurants within this work of fiction. The owners of these various products in this novel have been used without permission and should not be viewed as any sort of sponsorship on their part.

This book is licensed for your personal enjoyment only. This book may not be re-sold or given away to other people. If you would like to share this book with another person, please purchase an additional copy for each recipient. If you're reading this book and did not purchase it, or it was not purchased for your use only, then please return to your favorite book retailer and purchase your own copy. Thank you for respecting the hard work of this author.

This book is for my sister, Tammy.

*"They that love beyond the world cannot
be separated by it. Death cannot kill what
never dies."*
—Williams Penn

SERIES NOTE

The Stubborn Love Series consists of stories about the tough journey of the heart. They are companion novels and do not have to be read together to understand each story. All books focus on a different couple. Love isn't always easy and often can be painful, but if we open our hearts the rewards can be endless.

*Did you realize all the Stubborn Love Series book titles are inspired by songs?

STUBBORN LOVE

ONLY IN DREAMS

THE LUCKIEST

NEWSLETTER SIGNUP

Do you want to make sure you don't miss any upcoming releases or giveaways? Be sure to sign up for my newsletter at http://signup.wendyowensbooks.com/

PROLOGUE

I LOOK AT the clock again. I'm not sure what secrets I expect it to reveal. I've looked at it at least a hundred times in the last hour. 3:46 AM. Next, I look at my phone. This has become my ritual this evening. I have somehow become the girl I swore I would never be —the one waiting at home for the phone to ring.

When Christian and I moved in together three months ago, I thought the things that had been haunting him would somehow disappear. But, if anything, he has gotten worse. Even Emmie knows something is wrong. Though she does her best not to flaunt her and Colin's love fest in my face, I can't help but look at them and be reminded of all the things that are wrong between Christian and myself.

I've tried talking to him about his behavior. I tell him I can see that he's hurting; this approach only makes him angry. I know he's been drinking again, but every time I try and discuss it, he tells me to quit mothering him. Christ, I'm twenty-two years old. I shouldn't have to

1

worry about this stuff. Yet here I am. I look back at the clock. *Damn it Christian, where are you?*

The most horrible and terrifying things a person can imagine have been going through my mind. I've tried calling his cell several times, but now the mailbox is full. I mean, come on, a full mailbox? He would be furious if I treated him this way. When my agent called me earlier today and told me about an opportunity in Paris to model I turned him down flat. But now, with each passing minute that Christian disrespects me, without so much as a call, I am reconsidering my choice.

I love him; I know that much. And I used to be pretty sure he loved me. All of my model friends float from guy to guy and can't seem to understand what Christian and I have. It just doesn't make sense to them. Of course, it's not making very much sense to me either right now.

My mom was always in competition with me. First, with my dad, she would do everything she could to make sure he saw me as worthless. Eventually he couldn't stand being around her anymore. That was when she tried to use me as a weapon against him. I never blamed him, or maybe it was just that I no longer cared enough anymore about either of them to give a damn. But when my mom started making fun of me and telling all her boyfriends what a loser I was, I decided I wanted to be anywhere except in her house.

Then Christian walked into to my life. I wasn't looking for a man to rescue me; I was never that kind of girl. No, the great thing about him was that he was just as messed up and broken from the death of his parents, but some-how, we made sense together. At first we partied, and then when Christian realized after graduation that he didn't seem to know when to stop drinking, we simply fell into our next phase of life together. We could go out with all our friends, and because we had each other, Christian never needed to get wasted. He just liked being near me.

I'm not kidding myself. For the most part, I know he has always been about himself. He likes to look good, he likes to hang out with a certain crowd and attend the important events. When life gets to be too much you can find him at the gym, working on his massive muscles. Even Colin, his brother, is constantly teasing him about his manscaping. But even though he likes himself a lot, he's always managed to make me feel important and loved … until now.

I know if I could just get through to him, figure out what's causing all of these feelings he has been having, I could help him. But … I hear the key in the lock. I shift in my seat multiple times, unsure how I should handle this confrontation. My heart begins to race. Without thinking, I leap from the chair I am perched in and flop onto the couch, laying down with my eyes closed.

What am I doing? I think. *Am I really going to pretend like I'm asleep? Apparently so.*

I hear the door open, and Christian grunts as he fumbles with the lock, trying to remove his keys. Once the door is closed I listen for the lock to latch, but it doesn't happen. Instead I hear footsteps stumbling toward me—dragging across the floor. From the smell assaults my senses, I can tell he is extremely intoxicated.

I wait silently, assuming he's now staring at me, but I can't be sure. It's too late not to continue with the

3

charade. Then I hear more footsteps, and the bedroom door bash into the wall. Quickly I sit up and turn around, watching Christian stumble into the guest room. I can't believe what I'm seeing. Why on Earth would he be going in there?

I've had enough of the game. I want answers. I deserve answers. I hop to my feet and rush across the living room, poking my head in through the doorway Christian passed through moments ago. He is passed out, still fully dressed, including his shoes. Lying sideways across the bed, drool leaks from his mouth.

"Seriously?" is the only thing I can think to say. I want to cry; I want to throw things at him, and scream horrible things at him. But I don't do that. The last time I cried was when my dad left, and I decided nobody would ever get to see me do that again.

Christian mumbles an inaudible response, which then trails off into a snore.

"Christian? You've got to be kidding me." I try again, but I know he won't be waking up. Our talk will have to wait until morning. Unfortunately, sleep won't come as easily for me.

~

THE HOURS TICK by, and just as I suspected I've been unable to sleep. I lay in our bed at first, my face growing hot with anger. Then I clean, but I hate cleaning, so that doesn't last long. I think about calling Emmie around six o'clock, but that seems whiney and desperate. Not to mention the fact that I know most of what I tell Emmie she will tell Colin. If Colin knows Christian is getting wasted every night, it will start a huge fight between them, just giving him more ammo to use against me.

No, this is my problem, and I need to deal with it. By seven, I have come to the conclusion that maybe Christian isn't taking me seriously. I am always happy to clean up his messes, and it seems that he is well aware of it. Maybe now what he needs is some tough love. Maybe he needs to know I'm not going to be taken for granted anymore.

I waffle on this decision for sometime—I'm not one for idle threats—and before I make the ultimatum, I need to be certain I'll follow through. Poking my head into the guest bedroom one last time is all it takes. The room smells like a distillery. I realize now I love him enough to leave.

Packing my suitcase is harder than I thought it would be. I keep telling myself, *he won't let you leave, seeing your packed bags will be enough*. Going through the drawers, one by one, folding up my favorite thrift store treasures or photo shoot take home items, my mind drifts to Emmie.

She was a wreck when I met her. She didn't have any friends and was clearly suffering when it came to her fashion sense. I was the one who encouraged her to see how things would turn out with Colin. I was the example of happiness … wasn't I? How did I end up here? I missed my last two modeling jobs because Christian needed one thing or another. Now my agent had warned me that the calls would stop coming if I didn't start putting my best foot forward.

I gather the essential hair and makeup products I cannot live without and strategically place my suitcases against the wall, so that Christian will see them first thing when he wakes up. Then I wait, and wait, until I refuse to wait any longer.

Grabbing a wad of cash and my keys, I shove them into the pockets of my jumper and head to Ninth Street Espresso to grab a coffee. After a night of no sleep I need it, especially if I am going to have anything left in me for the shit storm that I know is going to happen when I get home. I keep having these moments where I think perhaps I'm overreacting, but as I recall the recent months, I quickly dismiss these notions.

"Hey Bill," I grumble as I approach the counter.

"Paige, where's Christian this fine morning?"

I debate how to answer. Christian and Colin are the owners of the space the coffee shop rents. While a huge part of me wants to unload on Bill and tell him exactly where Christian is, and exactly what my boyfriend can do to himself, I worry how this might affect their business relationship.

"Sleeping in." I decide to play it safe.

"Boy, he's got it rough, doesn't he?" Bill laughs. I feign a smile as I watch him prepare my latte.

"New tat?" I inquire, trying not to think about my good-for-nothing sloth of a boyfriend who is still passed out at home.

"How can you possibly notice that? Besides my girl-friend, you're the only one," Bill marvels, handing me my cup. Bill has tattooed sleeves on both arms; it is something I always take notice of while he makes my drinks. I've always been fascinated with body art—tattoos being a permanent fashion statement.

I pull out the wad of bills from my pocket, even though I already know Bill is going to wave me off. "On the house," he says.

I couldn't explain it to him. I had been taking free coffee from this place for as long as I could remember. And until today it was merely one of the perks of dating an owner of the building, but now, it feels dirty. I am so angry at Christian, the free coffee perk has become an unimaginable sin.

'No, I insist, you always give me freebies. I think we should start a policy where I at least pay for one out of a hundred," I joke, shoving the money further onto the counter.

"Your money is no good here, you know that," Bill replies lifting his hands up into the air.

Grabbing the wadded up bills, I drop them into the tip jar and walk out, flashing a smile over my shoulder. Bill is nice; it is too bad his landlord is such a dick head.

The walk home is the longest walk I have ever taken. I'm more than fine if it takes me the rest of the morning to get home. But, even with dragging my feet, a short fifteen minutes later, here I am, staring at the front door of my building.

I really do love this place, the ivy has begun to climb across the brick, and I am so thrilled I convinced Colin not to cut it back. The window boxes are overflowing with the springtime flowers I recently planted. As I fiddle with the keys, small rays of sunshine filter through the leaves of the big oak tree that is bursting from the seams of the green space on the sidewalk.

This place is home—one of the few places in my life that I feel like nobody can take away from me. Now that Christian and I live together, we can never undo the choice. He owns the building, so if anyone is going to move out, it is going to be me.

I shake my head, trying to force the idea out of my mind. There is no way it is going to come to that, I remind myself. Even if I left for a few days, Christian will realize how miserable he is without me, and I will be back —back in his arms. And not the arms of the guy passed out in the guest room. I'll be back with my Christian, the one I fell in love with as a teen.

I climb the stairs and enter the apartment. Looking around, I quickly realize Christian still isn't awake. I huff and push the wild strands of hair out of my face. I've waited long enough. This needs to happen.

Stepping into the guest room, I clear my throat, loudly. Christian lay in the exact same position as the night before, clearly undisturbed by my presence. Angrily, I rush over to his oversized, beefy body and give him multiple shoves. "Wake up. You need to wake up, now!"

"Huh," he says with a snort, wiping the drool gathering on his cheek with the back of his hand. "What's going on?"

He seems startled. He lifts his eyes, and squinting, tries to block out the light more with his hand.

"We need to talk," I say coolly.

I watch as he rolls his eyes and flops back down onto

the bed, clearly disgusted I woke him. "Can't this wait?" he moans.

"It has waited, all morning," I reply firmly.

"Paige, I'm serious, I feel like crap."

"That's not my fault."

"Jesus! I said not right now."

"Don't you dare raise your voice to me," I command, completely in shock that he would have the nerve to talk to me that way after putting me through hell last night. "For all I knew you were dead last night."

"I left my phone in Pete's car," Christian defends himself, not bothering to lift his head.

The answer does not appease me, only further infuriating me. "Pete Hannigan? The loser you said you were never going to see again, because all he does is hang out with a bunch of roadie losers at Kings and get drunk all the time? That Pete?"

"Yeah, that Pete!" Christian shouts, suddenly sitting up and glaring at me. I watch as he clutches his head, the sudden adjustment to his body and light obviously causing an intense pain. I'm not too ashamed to admit, I kind of feel he has it coming.

"What's going on with you?" I beg, fighting the urge to rush up and start shaking him wildly.

"Nothing," he grunts, standing and pushing past me to make his way into the bathroom. I walk into the living room, taking a seat on the chair that faces the door. He will have to look at me when he comes out. He will have to give me the answers I deserve.

I hear the flush, then a few seconds later he emerges from the doorway. He doesn't look at me, though. He makes his way to the kitchen sink and sticks his head under the faucet. After a good soaking, he lifts up, and while dripping water all over the floor, proceeds to question, "Where are the migraine pills?"

"Basket on the top of the fridge," I answer. I don't even know why. I have all this anger and fight inside of me, but all of the sudden I feel incredibly overwhelmed with sadness. He really doesn't care if I am upset. Perhaps I've been fooling myself about who he really is. As a girl I would watch my mom date these slime balls who would use her up until they were done and then throw her away. My stomach sinks as the idea I am exactly the same as her hits me.

"It's like a freaking jackhammer in my skull," he moans as he fidgets with the childproof cap, growing angrier.

I can't explain exactly what clicks for me in that moment. I stand and glide into the kitchen casually, grabbing the bottle from his hands, and pop the lid off with ease. I deal out a dose, replace the lid, and turn to pick up my bags.

"Where are you going?" he asks, noticing the luggage for the first time.

"I'm leaving," I say and make my way to the door, but before I can get there, he takes hold of my arm.

"Where? A job?" I can see it in his eyes. He knows what is happening as much as I do, but his voice almost sounds hopeful it really is just a modeling job.

"Yeah," I reply. I don't intend on taking the job in Paris, but when he asks me the question, the reply just slips out.

"When will you be back?" he inquires, his eyes shifting from my bags and then to my face repeatedly.

"I'm not coming back," I answer, a sigh of relief passing my lips. This isn't at all how I had expected the talk to go. I planned to complain and tell him how miserable I am. I would demand he change, or I would move out. But standing at the door, this isn't the tone at all. Christian is the kind of broken that I can't fix—he needs to fix himself.

"What the hell do you mean?" He is clearly becoming agitated very quickly.

"You know this has been coming for a long time. You need help, and I hope you get it, but I can't sit here and watch you self-destruct. I love you too much for that. I can feel the rush of emotions building up, but I know this goodbye can't be emotional, or it will scar both of us more than we can handle.

"Are you kidding me? I party too hard with the boys, I don't check in, and you're done."

"I—"

"I don't want to hear it, Paige. I'm sick of the drama. Get out then, if you're leaving, just leave," Christian snaps before turning his back to me.

I've never felt two such conflicting emotions at the same time. Part of me can see he is hurting. I want to scoop him up into my arms, pull him in close, and make it better. But then there is another part of me that loud and clear is telling myself, you deserve more than your mom and dad, you deserve more than him.

And then it happens, I says the words, "Goodbye, Christian." The door closes behind me, my first love on one side, the rest of my life on the other.

CHAPTER 1

our Years Later ...

I sit in the limo for a moment longer. The quietness consumes me. There's peace I haven't experienced in days. With all of the hustle and bustle of getting ready for the wedding, the last week has been a haze of meetings with the planner, caterer, DJ, along with countless others. I really can't understand why little girls dream of this day their entire lives. It seems like a terrible amount of work to simply declare to the public your plan to commit to one person for the rest of your life.

And then there is that thought. Committing to one person for the rest of your life. It never has seemed natural to me. Don't get me wrong, it's not like I'm promiscuous or anything. I can count the number of serious relationships I've had on one hand. When I find a guy, I don't mind committing, but for life?

"Miss, would you like me to get the door for you?" the handsome, young, and slightly rounded driver asks me.

I shake my head and quickly respond, "Oh, no, I'm fine." Pushing all the air from my lungs, I pull the lever and push open the heavy door, stepping out of my sanctuary.

Clementine spots me in what must be record time; I can only assume she was waiting for me. She waves her hands wildly, beckoning me. I'm not sure what I would do without her. When Emmie came to New York all those years ago, I never would have imagined that stranger I shared a taxi cab with would later become my best, and as it would seem, sometimes only, friend.

Walking in her direction, toward the front doors of the chapel, I glance over my shoulder. Traffic is whizzing by, people are living their lives, with no clue what is happening to me on this day.

"Will you hurry up?" Emmie yells, holding the large wooden door open. "Guests will be arriving soon, and we can't let them see you."

I wonder why that is. I mean, really, if my guests see me before I walk down the aisle, will it rip a hole in the space-time continuum? Why does it matter? I lower my head, staring at my sandal-clad feet as I approach.

"Are you all right?" Emmie asks. Leave it to her to always recognize when something is bothering me.

"Yeah, I'm fine, the hair dresser just took way longer than expected. I guess I'm just tired," I lie. Or maybe I'm not lying. I don't really know what's wrong with me. I simply feel sad. Do all brides feel this way on their wedding day? Maybe it's something that fades as soon as you see your groom waiting for you. I'm sure that's it. At least that's what I tell myself.

"She did take forever; you're so late. What was her deal?" Emmie begins, but she doesn't wait for me to answer. "Your dress is already in the changing room. I told your family I could help you get in it alone. I figured you preferred that."

There it is again, the reason I love her. You can't actually say the words, 'I can't stand my family. Can you please keep that group of toxic crazies away from me?' Emmie just knows.

I follow Emmie quietly into the old building, marveling at the marble floors as we enter. The detailing is one of the reasons I fell in love with the chapel in the first place. Staring at the back of Emmie's head, I notice how elegant her up-do is. Her often frizzy and somewhat out of control, dingy blonde hair has somehow been tamed into a crisp and clean sweep of petite curls. I smile, thinking of Em and Colin's wedding.

It was the perfect affair for the two of them. A country wedding at the hippie commune where Em's mom lives suited them. Well, I'm not sure if it is officially a commune, but that's what Em calls it. Emmie and Colin had the aisle for the wedding on one of the paths in the orchard, the number of guests very small, an intimate and perfect affair. Seemed like perfection to me. I wanted something just like it. I suppose I would have if my groom's family hadn't stepped in.

The Grove grew on me though, as did Em's mom. I often find myself wishing she were my own mother. My mother is the last thing I want to be thinking about right now. It took six months to even convince myself to invite her to my wedding.

Honestly though, all I care about is the dress. When it comes down to it, they can have the rest. My life revolves around fashion these days, and it simply doesn't seem right I release my own line and not design my wedding dress. It was a labor of love really—the massive amounts of hand-applied sheer fabrics in various shades of creams, ivories, and any other antique variation of white.

Stepping into the small room, the first thing my eyes move to is my dress. There it is, in all its glory. The grandmother of the groom tried pressuring me to wear a long train and gaudy veil. Clearly, she did not know with whom she was up against. *I* was in charge of what I would be wearing down the aisle.

Emmie is talking, but her words seem to fade into the background. I watch as my dear friend reaches up and pulls the garment I sank so many hours into preparing from the hanger with great care. She unfastens the hidden clasp on the side, just as I remove the last piece of clothing from my petite frame. I lift my arms over my head, closing my eyes. I don't want to see the dress until it's completely in place and revealed to me.

"Oh Paige—" Emmie gasps.

"What is it?" I inquire, now alarmed, spinning around to face the full-length mirror.

"You're stunning," Emmie replies, staring over my shoulder at the reflection. My heart sinks—I do feel beautiful—and my hands begin to sweat.

"Stay here, I'm going to see if they've begun seating," Emmie instructs.

"Where am I going to go?" I joke, truly reminding

myself there is nowhere to go. I am here, committed to this. And damn it, I am getting married today.

As I stare at my reflection, my mind is flooded with memories. I think of Emmie again, her happily ever after I had so envied. Unfortunately, my thoughts shift to my mother again. I lost count of her husbands and fiancés years ago. She always told me she just wasn't lucky at love. I worry again that I am a product of her and will follow the same path of heartbreak and ruin that she did.

I'm not sure how long I stand in that small room, looking at a woman in the mirror I barely recognize. My hair, after hours in a styling chair being straightened with a flat iron, is twisted up into a very elegant hair knot. I wanted a much more natural look, but this is nice, too, and I have far too many other things on my mind to complain.

I pick at my fingernails, the thick coat of shellac something I'm not used to, but it doesn't chip, so I simply rub the foreign layer on my usually unpolished nails, and accept it as a necessary inconvenience. I turn and look at the box on the floor, next to the chair, opening it carefully.

I wanted a handmade and vintage feel throughout the entire event, and my bouquet was no exception. I peer into the white box and marvel at the beauty of the paper flowers. A fashion designer I studied under for a few months is known for creating garments from hand-stained layers of paper. Using various colors, she rolled hundreds of small squares of paper together, sculpting a bouquet that can only be described as a piece of art.

"Hey beautiful, you ready?" I hear Colin's voice from

the doorway. Considering I haven't seen my father since I was a little girl and none of the men my mother ever hooked up with can be considered father figures, I chose Colin to walk me down the aisle.

"As I'll ever be," I reply with a smile, scooping up the paper bouquet in my hand and stepping forward to take a hold of his arm.

The door swings open the rest of the way, and I emerge from the closet-sized room. Emmie is waiting for us at the huge entry into the sanctuary, a smile on her face stretching from ear to ear. She rushes over to me, kisses my cheek, and offers words of encouragement in an attempt to soothe my nerves. I know it is in vain—my nerves will not be tamed—it's simply who I am.

"I love you," I say finally. A true and honest statement, the purest thing I can muster in that moment. We walk together, stopping just before the double doors, the light from the stained glass windows dancing across our skin. My eyes shift, and I watch a purple glimmer on my elbow. I stare as it slowly shifts down my arm, settling on my wrist.

There on my wrist I stare at the tattoo, which reads, 'I just might take the chance.' Quickly, I drop my arm, not wanting the words to haunt me on this day. I glance over at Colin, hoping he didn't catch me looking at the physical reminder of his brother. He doesn't seem to notice.

The music begins, my heart beating harder. I feel my eyes go wet, and I swallow deeply. Emmie squeezes my arm before saying, "See you at the other end."

I smile again; my face is starting to hurt. Faceless ushers close the doors, and Colin and I take our place for the big reveal. "It's almost time," he comments, looking down at me. I wonder if he can see how scared I am. "I promise, once you get down there, it's a piece of cake. It'll be gone before you know it, so savor every second."

I'm not sure how I feel about what he just said. I keep questioning myself, unsure if the way I'm feeling is normal. Does anyone really deserve to be with someone as messed up as me until death? I mean, wow, death. Doesn't anyone else think that is a terribly long time?

The doors open, and the noise in the sanctuary shifts as everyone stands and turns to look at me. I don't look at any of their faces. In my head, I keep telling myself over and over again, 'You can do this. Just keep smiling, keep smiling, keep smiling.'

Colin takes a step forward, pulling me along. The march feels like it takes forever. I wonder how long the aisle is and come to the conclusion it must be some sort of Guinness World Record for aisle lengths. I manage to make it the entire way without making eye contact with a single guest.

Instead, I focus my gaze at then end of the aisle. Emmie's smile is beaming back at me, and my heart grows warm. My eyes shift to the minister. His hair is black, the black that looks fake and shiny, so you know he must have a full head of gray he's covering up.

At last, I allow myself to look at him, there, waiting for me. I feel my heart begin to ache when our eyes meet, a tear rolling down his cheek. His eyes glisten with an expression of pure joy. I can't help but smile a huge, toothy grin as I take in his mess of sandy, untamed curls on top of his head. My Henry, the last thing he ever thinks about is fashion or grooming. It is always clear, though, that I am the first thing he thinks about.

Before I know it, Colin has handed me off to my soon-to-be husband, and the minister is speaking the words that will unite us forever as husband and wife. I am reassured in those passing moments that I am, in fact, doing the right thing. This man is a creature unlike any I've ever known. He is wiser and kinder than I could ever hope to be, and I'm better for being with him.

The pastor calls out to the crowd, as a formality, "If anyone has any reason why this couple should not be joined in matrimony, let them speak now." Soon, Henry will kiss me, and I will be his bride.

"I do," a voice calls out powerfully from the audience. My breath catches in my throat as I spin wildly to find Christian peering back at us. The crowd erupts into whispering assumptions. "She can't marry him because she still loves me!" he shouts.

My head is swimming, and I think I might vomit. I look back at Henry whose eyes are no longer filled with joy. Now I see pain staring back at me. My heart aches—this can't be happening. I open my mouth, but nothing comes out. The organ begins playing an ominous pitch, and I gasp as I wake up.

I am drenched in sweat. My heart is racing. I look next to me. Henry sleeps soundly. "It was a dream, just a dream," I tell myself.

CHAPTER 2

I WAKE UP, reach out, and run my hand across the sheets next to me to find they're cool to the touch. Like usual, Henry has gotten up long before me. During the early dating phase of our relationship, I never realized this about him. Usually when I would wake up, I'd find his eyes peering down at me. This made me uncomfortable the first few times I caught him doing it, but by the third or fourth time, something about it became almost comforting.

Once we moved in together, this habit slowly changed, and I began to see the Henry that is restless. Where I will, without much thought, sleep 'til noon on a Saturday morning, Henry can't sleep in, no matter how late he is up the night before. While I miss his warm body next to me in the morning, I can't complain, because he is always ninja-like in his exiting skills, allowing me to rest as long as my heart desires.

I sit up and reach for my robe, smiling as I think about Henry. When I first moved in, he never realized why I always wore his t-shirts to bed. I've always lived like a college student. I don't waste money on sexy pajamas, oh no, my funds are reserved for real clothes or going out. Once I moved in, my nighttime wardrobe became evident to him. He could see I was embarrassed by the revelation, so we spent the entire day shopping together. I now have more gowns and robes than I can ever possibly wear.

It's odd that something so simple can make me feel so sophisticated. I don't come from money like Henry. Everything I have in life I clawed out and grabbed onto for myself. To spend money on such luxurious, and in my mind, frivolous things, is hard to accept in some ways, but empowering in others. Henry is always good about sharing his wealth without flaunting it, a rare quality I've discovered over my lifetime. I can't say the same for his grandmother—ugh—it is far too early in the morning to think about that woman.

Speaking of too early, what time is it? I glance at the clock on Henry's side table. 9:38. I raise my eyebrows, impressed I haven't slept the Saturday away.

I slip my feet into the cozy shoes next to my bed and make my way into the kitchen. Being back in New York, after spending the last six months in Paris was unsettling at first, but it hasn't taken Henry and I long to fall back into a comfortable routine. When I first left for Paris, he sent me images of all the possible condo choices in Manhattan. Part of me wishes I could have been here for the process, but thanks to Henry, I got to feel like I was a part of it all from afar.

I have Henry to thank for most things in my life right now. He got me the apprenticeship under one of my favorite designers, and now I'm about to have my very own runway show. It's still hard to believe my own designs will be out in the world.

When I walk into the kitchen, I catch sight of Henry sitting at the breakfast table near the window, thumbing through the pages of his paper, sipping a cup of coffee. I stop dead in my tracks, drinking in the picture of him. His sandy hair is tousled; I smile as I see him clench his jaw. This is something he does as he reads the financial section. Just the hint of some facial hair casts a shadow on his jaw line—a rare sight as Henry is always clean-shaven.

My breath catches in my throat as he looks over at me, a smile spreading across his handsome face and a slight twinkle in his blue eyes. Oh, those blue eyes. I still remember the first time I saw them. It was like getting lost in a vast ocean. They swallowed me up, and their power has never released me.

"Good morning beautiful," Henry says. That has become his new normal. Every morning when I walk out for breakfast, he greets me with those words. My heart still floods with warmth when I hear it.

"Morning," I reply, walking over to him and pressing my lips against his forehead. When I pull away I see him wince slightly. "Are you all right?"

He nods. "Yeah, it's this headache. I just can't seem to shake it."

"Have you taken anything for it?" I ask, walking over to pour myself a cup of coffee.

"Yeah, but none of it seems to work," he replies, glancing back at the pages of his paper.

I grab one of the croissants from the plate on the

counter and shove it in my mouth, using my free hands to add cream and sugar, before making my way over to Henry, taking a seat across from him. I pull off a piece of the delicate pastry and set the remaining piece on the table.

I see Henry eye the plate-less food. Though I know things like this annoy him, I also know he will never say it to me. I grab a napkin from the wire holder in the center of the table and place it as a barrier between the table and my food. This seems to please him as a smile tickles the corners of his mouth. I find his various quirks endearing.

"You don't take care of yourself," I insist, a fact I have argued since early in our relationship. "You never shut off."

"Sure I do," Henry dismisses my statement.

"Oh yeah? It's a Saturday, and what are you doing right now?"

"Sitting across from the most beautiful fiancée a man could ever hope for."

"Boy, you're laying it on thick this morning."

Henry laughs, setting the paper to the side. "I know, and I'm sorry. I'm off work. The last thing I should be doing is reading the financials."

"Oh yeah?" I taunt. "Then what exactly should you be doing?'

"How about we spend the entire day together?" Henry suggests.

"That sounds perfect," I reply "But ... I have crazy amounts of work to do for the show. It's ten weeks away, and I haven't even sketched all of the designs."

Henry leans forward and grabs me with his strong and

powerful grasp, pulling me into his body and wrapping his arms around me. "I see how it is," he teases. "You tell me I work too hard, but who can't take a day off now?"

"Hey wait," I laugh, then chime defensively. "The only reason I have to work so hard is because somebody, whose name I shall not mention, committed me to a show with a four-month deadline."

Henry nibbles on my neck, and I squirm, the ticklish sensation overwhelming me. It's pointless to struggle though; his embrace is far too strong for me to break free.

"You're welcome," he says at last, then continues. "You also have a wedding to plan, if I do recall."

I stiffen. The mention of the wedding reminds me of the dream I had the night before ... the dream of Christian. Why did I have that dream? I somehow always manage to do this to myself, when I find happiness, I inevitably find some way to sabotage it.

"Are you all right?" Henry asks, sensing the shift in my body. His arms fall to his side, releasing me, and he stares, waiting for a response.

"I'm fine," I lie, slinking back to my seat, doing my best not to look into those blue eyes. I'm not fine—I feel terrible—this man who loves me with everything in him deserves to have someone who isn't as messed up as I am. Someone who doesn't dream about a man she hasn't been with for over four years. I can't lose Henry. I need him. He is more than the best chapter of my life; he's helped me figure out who and what I want.

"Baby, something's wrong. Come on, you can tell me," he pushes, stretching out an arm and placing his hand on top of mine. His fingers are masculine yet slender. I always enjoy tracing them with my tiny, pale fingertips. With his other hand he reaches up and tucks a stray wiry auburn strand of hair behind my ear, and lifts my chin with his fingertips, forcing me to look at him. "I love you. Now tell me."

For a brief second I think about telling him, but men have a jealous habit and don't exactly understand. I don't know what the dream meant, but it probably doesn't mean anything. Christian and I have been over for quite some time. There are no lingering feelings, in fact, I rarely even think of him now.

"I think I'm just feeling overwhelmed. There are so many distractions here, and it feels like I'll never be able to get it all done in time," I say, shifting the focus away from the dream I don't want to talk about.

"Well, what can I do? Do you need more help with the wedding? Maybe I can take some days off," Henry offers. And there it is, that guy who can't stand for me to be unhappy. I'm the center of his world, and he is never afraid to let me know it. I wish I were as brave.

"I know you're busy with work. You're taking three weeks off for our honeymoon. You don't have any more time to give, but I do appreciate it," I reply, gripping his hand firmly in my own.

"What about a girlfriend? Can you enlist one of them to help you?" Henry suggests.

I burst out laughing, and he peers back at me, puzzled. "I wouldn't exactly call any of my friends in New York helpful. Emmie is the only one I can count on, but with her and Colin living in Texas now, that's not going to happen."

I watch Henry's face twist, and then suddenly it lights up. "It's settled then."

Shaking my head, I ask, "What's settled?"

"Today we spend the day together, tomorrow, you're on a plane to Texas."

"What? I have too much to do, I can't."

"Exactly. You have too much to do. Emmie will be the perfect solution. I'll ship you everything you need for the fashion show, you work on that while Emmie helps with the wedding planning. It's only ten weeks, Paige. We'll talk every night; I'll fly down for visits when I can. In ten weeks you'll be home, the show will be amazing, another week after that we'll be married, and I'll be caught up on my work, which means I can leave the firm for three whole weeks in paradise."

I tilt my head and think about the suggestion for a moment. "Well, when you put it like that."

Henry hops to his feet and takes my hand. "Then I say we start our perfect day of togetherness in the bedroom … without all these clothes."

"Henry Wallace, what has gotten into you?" I giggle, gladly allowing myself to be led.

"Oh, I think I have a lot of surprises in store for you," Henry snarls, and I feel myself grow warm within.

∾

CHAPTER 3

AKING A DEEP breath, I soak in the moment—balancing the bath towel my hair is wrapped in on top of my head. Henry is in the shower, and my thoughts drift to our morning of passion, before the growling of my stomach reminds me that such actions require sustenance. Quickly, I run through what I need to take care of—pack for my extended trip, book my flight, make arrangements to have my fabrics shipped to Emmie's gallery, and it might be nice to call my dear friend and let her know she's about to have a house guest for the next couple months.

I reach over and pick up the phone from my night-stand, ignoring the numerous and annoying Facebook notifications, and flip to my contact list. My heart skips a beat as I press Em's name.

I listen as the phone rings—one, then two—finding myself growing impatient, missing the voice of my sweet Emmie. "Hello," she finally answers, sounding out of breath.

"Hey darling! It's Paige," I reply.

"I know, there's this great thing nowadays called caller I.D."

"Oh, how I've missed that bitchy streak."

"Sorry, the baby kept me up all night," Emmie offers.

"How is beautiful little Olivia?"

"She's great, it's her mom who might be losing her mind. She sleeps all day and then is up all night."

"Sounds miserable," I reply honestly.

"You know what, I hardly ever get to hear your voice anymore, so let's not talk about how I get no sleep. What's going on with you?" Emmie asks. I can hear her trying to shift her tone. I wish I could reach through the phone and give her a supportive hug.

"I have big surprise."

"Let's see, your last surprise was that you had been offered a show of your own clothing designs, and the surprise before that was that Henry had gotten you a design apprenticeship in Paris, shortly after proposing with a big ass diamond ring. With you girl, I can't imagine what your next surprise will be."

I smile, so used to the excitement of my life that I forget how amazing of a dream I am living. "Well, it's not quite in the same family of those other things, but I think equally as exciting."

"Well, don't keep me in suspense, what's the surprise?" she presses.

"You're going to have a house guest," I answer excitedly.

"Huh?"

"I'm coming to Texas, girl!" I exclaim, surprised to be met by silence on the other end of the line. "Em?"

"Yeah, I'm— I'm here."

"Did you hear me?" I ask, certain she must not have, or I would have heard it in her reaction.

"Yeah, I heard you. I'm just confused, I guess."

"What do you mean?"

Emmie pauses, choosing her words carefully. "You have a fashion show coming up in a few months, not to mention a wedding. How can you possibly come for a visit?"

"That's why I'm coming. I was stressing out this morning about how I have no friends to help me with the wedding planning here, and I think Henry knows I've been missing you guys so much that he told me I should go down there and finish my show in Bastrop."

"That's … great," Emmie says, though I can sense the uncertainty in her voice.

"All right, lay it on me, what's up?" I push.

"I don't know if it's the best time to head down here, sweetie. Between the gallery and Olivia, we barely have time for ourselves, let alone a houseguest. I mean—it's not that I wouldn't love to see you, I just think it might be a distraction for you."

"Nonsense. Ten weeks down in sleepy town Texas is just what the doctor ordered. And besides, I can't wait to get my hands on Liv, which will free up some time for you and Colin to be alone. Just no details, please."

"Well, I guess." Emmie still seems hesitant.

"Ten weeks with your bestie. What more could you ask for? Unless there's some other reason I shouldn't come. Is there something else, Emmie? Are you and Colin doing all right?"

"Other than being sleep deprived, we're great. You're right, this will be good."

"Perfect, I'll book my flight into Austin for tomorrow."

"I'll have Colin pick you up, so just text me the time your flight gets in."

"No, don't be ridiculous, you guys have your hands full there; I'll just take a taxi."

"Are you sure?" she asks.

The last thing I want to do is sit in a vehicle—alone— with Christian's brother for an hour. A taxi will be best for everyone. "Absolutely, it's not a big deal."

"Well, now I am getting excited."

"Me too. I still can't believe you moved to Texas."

"Oh, Paige, you're going to love it here."

"I don't know about that, Em. You know I'm a city girl. But I do know I am looking forward to spending time with some of my favorite people." I hear the water shut off in the bathroom.

"You can actually see the stars at night here."

"Well, I hope it's as enchanting as you've described. Henry just got out of the shower, so I need to get ready. He's got a togetherness day planned for us before I leave."

"You two are so cute," she comments.

"And you're such a dork," I joke before we exchange our farewells, and I hang up the phone. It's official; I'm headed to Texas. Part of me feels apprehensive., though It feels like maybe Em isn't as excited about the idea as I am, and I definitely don't want to be an imposition. Forcing the thought from my mind, I decide I will make sure I am nothing of the kind when I get down there.

CHAPTER 4

"FOLKS, WE'VE BEGUN our descent into Austin, where the current weather is a beautiful seventy-seven degrees. We will be at the gate in about twenty minutes. As our flight attendants begin to prepare the cabin for arrival, we'd like to thank you for flying with us today." I stare out the window to my right, the land below still patchy through the clouds.

Glancing to my left, the oversized gentleman, who has been dropping bits of food onto my leg for the majority of the flight, is unhappy that the flight attendant has asked him to stow away his carryon bag for the descent. I regret not allowing Henry to book me in first class, as he had suggested before I left.

One of the few times I'd actually flown first class was when I met Henry. I had taken the modeling job in Europe and, after eighteen months of non-stop travel and shows with the agency, I was flying home. I'd been one of their most dedicated girls, never turning down an event, no schedule too crazy for me. I didn't have anyone waiting back at home, so there was no reason for me to stop pushing full speed ahead. Much to my delight, the agency had upgraded my flight home to first class as a thank you.

The idea of oversized, comfortable seats for a massively expensive upgrade fee had always seemed like a ridiculous concept to me. However, anyone who has been on one of those exhausting overseas flights would agree, an extra comfy seat can feel like a necessity after the fourth hour in the air.

By chance, Henry had the seat next to me. I didn't notice him at first, honestly. I had spent so much time traveling I barely noticed anything those days. He was the one who struck up some small talk with me. He was terrible at it.

"Frequent flyer?" I laugh as I remember the words. Had he not been so handsome I might have even asked to change seats. We talked the entire flight home, and boy was I glad I didn't move. The last time I could recall having such an intense connection with someone was when I met Emmie.

Henry ran an investment firm that had been his father's. Most of the men I had dated weren't very forth-coming with details about their lives. In fact, they didn't really seem to care much about my life either. They liked to party, and they liked the idea of having a Paris runway model on their arm.

On that flight I found out Henry's dad died when he was in his fifties from a massive heart attack and, as a result, he did his best to eat healthy and exercise regularly. His grandmother on his father's side came from old money, and she hated his mother, who was nothing more than a gold digger in her eyes. His mother was madly in love with his father, and after he died, she quit eating and talking—she simply gave up on living.

I remember seeing tears in his eyes when he told me about his mom, but he never did cry. There was a sorrow behind them that made me ache for this stranger. She found out she had cancer, but refused any kind of treatment. He had been begging her to do something, but it was like she was ready to die. He was actually headed home after consulting a specialist in Europe when we met.

I'm glad we met when we did. I was still able to meet her, which I know meant a lot to Henry. She was a delicate woman, soft spoken, with a small stature. Her nearly white blonde hair always draped around over one shoulder, and her skin was pale and soft. It was a joy watching her with Henry. I could see he made her happy. I even tried to convince her once, for Henry, to get treatment.

She told me one day, I would love so deeply that the loneliness of being apart from that man would hurt so that nothing could fill the void. I didn't tell her I had already experienced emptiness like that, a hole left by my first love, Christian. I just hoped lightning could strike twice.

And she was right. I found that thing I needed, the thing she was certain no longer existed for her in this world. Henry was who I needed to put Christian behind me.

I had shared things with Henry on that flight that I had never shared with anyone. I told him about my mother and how I was always competing for attention with the men she was dating. The only people in my life who had known about the drama between that woman and myself were Christian and Emmie. But here I was, within hours of meeting Henry, and I was spilling my entire life history with all of its dysfunction and misery. He never made me feel broken; he just listened.

He listened to everything I had to say. He wanted to hear about how I loved clothes—clothes that make you feel beautiful and sexy, while managing to let you feel comfortable. It was on that flight that I admitted I wanted to be a fashion designer, not a model. I wanted to make clothes that made people feel good. His response had been so simple. He asked me why I wasn't doing that then, and I had no answer.

The night that plane landed he invited me to dinner, and I couldn't imagine answering anything other than yes. I didn't want our time together to end. We ended up talking at the restaurant until the waiters told us they were closing up. He wanted to know about Emmie and Colin, who at the time had recently gotten engaged. Six months later he was my date to the big event.

"Please return your seat to the upright position," I hear the voice request to the left of me. With a huff, the portly and grumpy man next to me complies.

"Almost there," I tell myself.

Henry had even made me feel comfortable enough to talk about Christian. I was a little worried that Christian was going to make a scene at Colin and Emmie's wedding, but much to my surprise, he avoided me like the plague. I shouldn't be shocked, considering how we left things.

Christian is the past, though; it's been over four years since I walked out of our New York apartment. He didn't come after me, he didn't call me, and it was painfully clear I had cared for him much deeper than he ever cared for me. For a while Emmie would update me on where he was or what he was doing, but eventually that stopped. I didn't want to know anymore.

"Can you believe this woman?" the man next to me grumbled in my direction. I flashed a half-smile and then looked back out the window. I'm not really sure what kind of crazy the man is, but I really want nothing to do with him.

I watch as the earth comes rocketing towards us, the plane rumbling as the landing gear descends. I've flown more than most people I've met, and still the landing unsettles me. Something doesn't seem natural to me about falling from the air so quickly and colliding with the earth at those speeds.

Closing my eyes, I clench my fists, holding my breath and preparing myself for the touch down. Once contact is made, this somehow gives crazy man next to me the okay to try and start a conversation.

"Scared of flying or something?" he asks with a snort.

I shrug my shoulders, hoping he will take this response for how it is meant—a signal to shut up and leave me alone.

"It doesn't bother me at all," he informs me, clearly not getting the message.

He continues rambling about numerous things of which I care nothing about, including the fact that he has three cats who are probably making a mess of his apartment right now, because they can't stand being away from him. Suddenly I feel very sad for these cats I have never met.

At last we are locked into the gate, and I begin counting down the moments until I will be out of this capsule with cat man and on my way to see Emmie and my honorary niece, Olivia, whom I affectionately refer to as my little Olive.

I wait patiently for the man next to me to gather his bags and stand up. As he does, a waterfall of crumbs and uneaten bits of food tumbles to the floor. He doesn't seem to notice. Raising a hand to my mouth, I do my best not to vomit as the smell of onions fills the air.

"It was nice talking to you. Maybe I'll see you around," he says as he turns and makes his way down the aisle. It never ceases to amaze me how someone who doesn't seem to bother with the most basic things in life, like bathing, would think I would have any interest in carrying on any kind of conversation. Yet, these characters always manage to seek me out.

I stand, brushing myself off and grabbing my purse, taking my time—at the annoyance of the passengers behind me—to ensure the creepy, smelly, cat guy gets some distance ahead of me. I sigh, relief washing over me that soon I'll be back with Emmie.

～

CHAPTER 5

*W*HEN I CLIMB into the taxi I never expect to get a history lesson from the driver. Apparently he is an expert of Bastrop and is thrilled to impart his knowledge during the thirty-minute ride there. With just over seven thousand residents, the little town apparently succeeds in having that small town feel, while remaining part of what's considered Austin's metropolitan area.

At times, I find myself wondering if the Bastrop tourism office might pay this guy for his dedicated praise of the town. He proceeds to inform me at one point that they even have a Wal-Mart. To which, of course, I answer, "Thank goodness, I can't live without my Wal-Mart." I think my sarcastic tone might have escaped the poor fellow.

Quite honestly, though, after all the fast-paced, pushy New York cabbies, it is kind of nice to have a guy that really enjoys his job, as well as the area where he lives. He even makes me promise to try the Roadhouse, a restaurant off State Highway 21 during my stay.

Emmie and Colin had decided, when they were expecting Olivia, they didn't want to raise kids in the city. She wanted the small town Midwest feel she had grown up in as well as a strong art community so they could open a gallery. After extensive research, and a lot of visits to various towns, they settled on Bastrop.

It is hard to believe they have lived here for a little over a year now, and this is my first time visiting. They made such frequent trips back to New York in the beginning, as Colin was liquidating a lot of his properties, there never seemed a need for me to head south. Then came my apprenticeship in Paris, and before I knew it, I was back and living in a penthouse with Henry while Emmie had her family in Texas. Sometimes it feels like the entire world lay between us, and I miss her being just across the living room.

As we pull down the main strip I can hardly believe what I am seeing. It is like I'm on the set of a movie. I've seen places like this on television, but I suppose I never processed that they actually existed. Could it be? Places like Mayberry were out there? The street is quiet, with a handful of cars parked on either side.

"This is downtown?" I ask in disbelief.

"Sure is."

We roll past one small building painted in a muted teal color, and across the stone building I read, 'Chamber of Commerce.' Just past that building the cab pulls into a parking spot. Opening the door, I step out and look around. On the far side of the street I see numerous galleries, antiques shops, a quaint bakery, a florist, even an old-fashioned looking drug store.

Turning and walking around to meet the cab driver, currently removing my bags from the trunk, I hand him the fare with a generous tip, thanking him for the information-packed ride. Throwing my travel bag over my shoulder, I roll the oversized suitcase behind me. When I come around the other side of the cab and see the small, beautifully carved sign that reads Bennett Family Art Gallery a smile emerges, covering my face from ear to ear. I am here. This is it. I am about to see Emmie, and she will bring the calm back into my life I have been missing.

To the left of the gallery is a picket fence leading to a courtyard, along with a wooden sign, similar to the one for Em's gallery. It reads, Bennett Woodworking. I should have guessed Colin couldn't slow down enough to just be a dad and run the gallery after being a property investor in New York. I am a little surprised, however, Em hadn't told me about his latest venture.

I hear the driver pull away, and I pull my bags behind me, fumbling for the front door, finally grasping it with my partially free hand. I yank the door open, a service bell above me chimes, and that's when it happens. I hear something I never expected to.

"Hey Christian," a man shouts from across the street. Instinctively, I turn my head and look. He's already looking at me as the man approaches him. He looks different than the last time I saw him, but it's Christian. His shoulders seem broader; his hair is longer, the dark strands falling into his eyes. He has a few days worth of beard growth on his jaw line.

He begins talking to the man who had called out his name, constantly looking over at me as he does. I feel a pain in my chest and a fluttering in my stomach. I panic; I don't know what to do. The taxi is gone—I can't run—there's nowhere to go.

"Paige?" I hear Emmie's voice as she emerges from the back room.

I turn and look at my friend. Her hair is twisted up into a bun, and she's wearing glasses, which I've never seen her in. Sweet Olivia is on her hip, no longer bald, no longer my Olive head. Tugging on the luggage, I push my way into the door. I don't look back at him.

"Colin, Paige is here!" Emmie shouts. Colin rushes out from a hidden corridor and across the room, scooping me up into that big brother-like embrace I'd forgotten about. He has always looked out for me, even when I was a kid, and suddenly that same feeling comes back. My bags fall to the floor as I wrap my arms right back around him, squeezing as if he were about to slip away. It's hard not to see Christian in him, but I do my best not to think about his brother. His brother who was right outside on the street, the last place he should be.

Colin sets me down, grabbing my bags as if they were empty. He carries them off out of sight, as I open my arms, wrapping them around my sweet Emmie and Olivia. "She's so big!" I exclaim.

"Momma," Olivia squeals in delight from the excitement in the room.

"Oh my God!" I gasp. "She sounds even cuter in person than over Skype."

Emmie smiles and holds Olivia with one arm while wrapping her other around me. "I missed you so much."

"I missed you, too," I reply, looking around the room, recognizing several works by my friend. "Oh, Em, this place is incredible. Your description doesn't do it justice."

Emmie nods, glancing at all she has accomplished over the past year. "We like it. We're up to thirty consignment artists, and the list seems to be growing all the time. The online orders for my work keep Colin pretty busy with shipping."

"Well, that and the woodworking, but why didn't you tell me?" I inquire.

Emmie doesn't reply. I look at her face as it twists into a horrific expression.

"Em? Are you okay?"

"I wanted to tell you so many times."

"That Colin started his own business? Why would I—"

Emmie is shaking her head no, and suddenly it all makes sense. It feels like someone punched me in the gut. She can see it on my face. I can tell. The woodworking business isn't Colin's; it is his brother's.

"When you called, I tried to tell you, but I just didn't know how," she pleads.

"How long has he been here?"

"He came to help us move in and get set up. He never left."

"What?" I cry.

"He said he wanted to be an uncle. After a couple months, he started making furniture to sell at the local markets, and then they were so popular he—"

43

"I need to lay down," I interrupt her, my head now spinning.

"Colin!" Emmie shouts, beckoning him from the room he had disappeared into.

I don't even remember walking to the guest room. I vaguely recall some stairs, a green door, Colin saying some words, and then I am alone, in a room, my plan to seek refuge from my haunting past, from that horrible dream, coming undone.

CHAPTER 6

I SIT ON the bed, staring at the floral wallpaper for quite sometime. I remember Emmie knocking on the door, but I didn't respond, I didn't move, I just sat there, staring. I'm not even sure what I was thinking about, my thoughts had been jumping all over the place, all morning. Should I call Henry and tell him that Christian is in town? Would that make it into a bigger deal than it actually is? Is it a big deal? Christian is my past, which is long over. Perhaps it is a non-issue.

At some point I must have laid down and dozed off, because now, the bright afternoon sun that had been flooding into the room, has shifted into a hazy cast of dusk. Standing, I grab the suitcases Colin had set inside the door for me. Taking a deep breath, I swallow hard. Tossing the larger bag on the bed and unzipping it, I decide this is a non-issue. I'm sure Christian could care less that I'm here, so I won't let it bother me either. After all, I'm happy now.

Looking around the room, I catch sight of a small,

hand-painted teal dresser that is pushed back into a window cubby. Grabbing a stack of my blue jeans, I walk over, pulling out the second drawer, and neatly place my items inside. With a little bit of wiggling and maneuvering, I shove the drawer back into place, falling against the top of the dresser, catching myself with my palms as I do.

Just outside the window, I stare into the quaint courtyard directly next to the shop. At the back of the courtyard was another building set back from the street some. Movement near the entrance of the small business catches my attention. I hold my breath at the sight of Christian. He lifts a log, placing it across a seesaw, random tools strewn about him. It reminds me of when I used to watch him working with his brother on their properties in New York. They were like artists with what they did with some of those rehabs.

Panic overwhelms me as Christian looks up to the window, locking me into his gaze. He is only wearing a tank top now with his tattered and well-worn jeans. He uses the back of his forearm to wipe the sweat away from his brow. The entire time, though, he doesn't take his eyes off me. Suddenly he smiles, and I find myself smiling back. Looking over, I realize I'm waving at him. Using my other hand, I pull my flailing arm down, which has developed a mind of it's own, and push myself away from the window.

Before I realize what's happening, the memories begin to play out before me, all the moments of our lives in New York—the happiness and laughter. I was okay with never seeing Christian again. I'd made peace with him no longer being a part of my life. *Damn it, he's not a part of my life.*

He's Colin's brother. Christian is part of their lives. He isn't here because of me, I tell myself. *He's here to be an uncle to his niece, and I shouldn't even be thinking about him.*

Frantically, I return to my suitcase, pulling out a sheer dress, then a lacy blouse, and a gorgeous vintage mini skirt. I make my way to the closet, hanging the clothes up with care. *Stop thinking about him, Paige. His strong shoulders, those muscles on his upper arms when they lifted that massive log, those eyes as they were staring back up at me. Henry! Henry has amazing blue eyes*, I remind myself sternly. *You love those eyes, the ones you get lost in. You can stare into them for hours while he talks about anything. Henry has the most amazing smile.* Then I remember Christian's smile. *The way one lip lifts higher on one side. That goofy, crooked smile with one deep dimple. That's something I used to get lost in, that dimple.*

My phone rings. I'm thankful for the interruption. I race across the room, grabbing it off the nightstand and look at the picture on the front. Henry, there he is smiling back at me. My heart starts to race. I take a deep breath, trying to calm myself before answering. I swipe my finger across the phone.

"Hi baby." My voice cracks a little.

"Hello beautiful," he responds, and the panic inside me calms, his voice a reminder of what I have now. "I guess you made it all right?"

"Sorry, I should have called."

"No, I'm sure you've had a ton of catching up to do with Emmie. Have you girls been going on non-stop?"

I pause, wondering if I should tell him about Christian again. "Actually, I fell asleep."

"You're kidding me? Are you feeling all right?" Henry asks, chuckling.

"Yeah, I set my bags down, and next thing I knew I was asleep," I answer honestly.

"I'm a little jealous. I tried to nap earlier, but I couldn't sleep without you next to me."

"You? Nap?" I question. "You never nap. Who is this?"

Henry laughs again. I've missed that laugh. He enjoys my sarcasm, which I love because that means I get to hear that laugh a lot. "Actually, I've had a headache I can't seem to shake. I thought a nap might do me good."

"Honey," I begin, my voice shifting to one heavy with concern. "You had a headache before I left."

"I know."

"That's not normal."

"It's fine. I've just not been taking as good of care of myself as I should. Someone keeps me up all night, not that I'm complaining. I'll give up sleep any day for that."

I realize I'm smiling.

"I miss you," he adds softly.

"Me too."

"I miss your body," Henry continues.

"Oh yeah?" I inquire, hoping for more, as I make myself comfortable on the bed.

"Yeah."

"And what exactly about my body do you miss?" I ask, eagerly awaiting the details.

"Your legs."

"You like my legs, huh?"

"Especially when they're wrapped around me. When I can run my hands down your soft back until they meet your ass. I love holding your amazing ass while you rock against me."

"Henry!" I squeal.

"What? I thought that's what you wanted," he replies in an innocent tone.

"You're going to make me fly back home tonight if you don't watch it."

"Don't tempt me."

"I love you." The words slide out of me effortlessly. It's not a part I'm playing—it's my life. In the back of my mind I am processing the idea. I'm okay with Christian being here, because I mean those words when I say them to Henry. The things I feel when I see Christian are hauntings from my past, and I can handle that, because I have Henry. And I love him.

"I love you, too. Can I call you tomorrow?" he asks.

"You better," I say, staring at the ceiling.

"Go hang out with your friend, have some fun tonight, and then get to work tomorrow," he instructs.

"Okay, you don't have to twist my arm. Promise you'll get some rest?"

"I'll do my best in this cold, lonely bed."

"Don't make me feel bad or anything," I gasp, acting as though I were hurt.

"You should feel bad. You're forcing me to get takeout for one. Do you know how pathetic that is?"

"Very," I say, taking in a deep breath. "Smells like I'll be having a home-cooked meal."

"Oh, you're so cruel."

"I try," I say before laughing wickedly.

"I miss you." His voice is now soft and sincere.

"I miss you, too."

"Goodnight."

"Goodnight, baby," I say, and then wait for him to hang up first.

~

CHAPTER 7

I WATCH IN amazement as Emmie and Colin scurry around one another. Their movements are like a dance—there is no music, but they're in harmony together. Colin grabs the baby bag, throwing it over his shoulder, while Emmie, with Olivia on her hip, grabs a couple snacks with her free hand. She spins, tossing them to Colin, who catches them effortlessly, placing them with the other items he has been collecting. Emmie wastes no time grabbing Olivia's favorite blanket, and Colin places the stroller on his spare arm.

"Now, you have our cell phone numbers, in case you need us," Emmie reminds me as if I were a clueless teenager.

"I'll be fine, I told you," I insist.

"I'm serious, if you need anything at all, just call one of us, but like I said, in the middle of the day during the week it's rare we get a lot of foot traffic, so I'm sure you won't even have to do anything," Emmie continues, clearly unsure about leaving the gallery completely in my hands for the afternoon.

"It's thirty minutes to the pediatrician and then thirty back, we should be home within a couple hours," Colin adds.

"Go!" I exclaim. "I've got this."

"All right, all right, we're going," Emmie says, lifting a hand defensively.

I watch out the kitchen window as Colin and Emmie pack Olivia, and the massive amount of objects it takes to care for her, into their Prius. It amazes me how much they have fallen into the family role. Even when Colin and Emmie met, I knew they would be a perfect pair, but if you would have told me five years later they would be married with a baby, I'm not sure I would have believed you.

The idea of commitment terrified Emmie, after such a tragic ending to her first marriage. Who could blame her? Colin was so patient, though. I've always thought of him like a big brother, but for him to treat her with so much understanding through their relationship only made me love him all the more. Eventually it became natural for her to let him love her. It was like an acceptance settled over her, she finally seemed to realize Colin wasn't going to turn into something else. He was being who he really was with her, and he was in it for the long haul.

I think the end of Christian's and my relationship was more of the shock for everyone. For the first year Emmie and Colin expected us to figure things out and find our way back to each other. Once I moved in with Henry, those assumptions seemed to fade away, slowly though.

There was a time even I thought Christian was my soul mate, but we eventually all have to grow up and realize that when we're young we can mold things into fairytales they're not. We romanticize situations, making more of something that doesn't exist.

Walking to the stove, I remove the screaming teakettle and pour the boiling water over the tea bag at the bottom of my mug. Just as I set the pot onto one of the cool burners, the bell in the front of the gallery rings, signally that the door has opened. *Yeah, this place is dead on weekdays; I didn't even have time for my tea to steep.* Staring at the mug, as I carefully carry the hot beverage out to the front counter and set it down, looking up to greet the customer, which I know I have no clue how to really do, but how hard can it be? It's not a customer looking back at me, though; it's Christian.

"What are you doing here?" The words escape my mouth before I can even process what I'm saying.

"Nice to see you, too," Christian laughs, both arms wrapped around a large package.

"Sorry, I didn't mean—" I begin, stopping myself to take a deep breath before continuing. "I wasn't expecting to see you. I thought you were a customer."

"Sorry to disappoint, but I do come bearing gifts," he replies.

My face contorts and twists into a look of puzzlement.

"Well, I hope it's a gift. I really have no idea what's inside, but it's addressed to you. I was picking up a delivery this morning, and they asked me to drop this off to the shop."

Shaking my head, I smile, realizing he was bringing

some of the design stuff Henry shipped down to me. "It's for work," I explain, moving out from around the counter and crossing the concrete floors to take the package from him. As I reach out and place my hands on the box, his skin brushes against me as he pulls away. I drop the box as I recoil from the brief interaction.

"Are you all right?" Christian asks, dipping low to pick up the package from the ground. Much to my dismay, I bend down at the same time to retrieve the dropped goods, causing our heads to smack into one another's.

We both stumble back, clutching our heads in pain. I grab a hold of the counter to steady myself. I realize Christian is wailing with laughter.

"I'm glad you find my pain so hilarious," I snarl.

Christian quickly approaches, scooping up the discarded package, placing it on the counter. "I'm laughing because I see you are just as graceful as you used to be."

"Hey!" I gasp, then laugh, realizing he's right. "How is it I can walk down a runway in four-inch heels, but damn it, anything else, and somehow I manage to hurt myself?"

"No clue. I suppose you're just gifted that way," Christian adds, gasping for breath between laughs, before a silence settles over the room. He quickly attempts to alleviate any awkward silence. "So, I hear you're not modeling anymore. Finally decided to hang your stilettos up?"

I examine Christian, quiet for a moment, trying to gauge what his sudden interest in me means. Then, convincing myself he is simply trying to be nice, I answer, "When you say it like that it sounds like I was a stripper."

He laughs again. "I've missed your sense of humor."

I feel my stomach flip as I wonder what else he has missed, then remember the original question. "My fiancé helped me get into fashion design."

"Yeah, I heard that, too."

"What? About the show? They told you?"

"Well, about that and about your engagement," he says, watching my face for a reaction. I give him none.

"At least one of us was told what was going on in the other's life."

"Huh?"

"Just you, and being here, and—" I hesitate, and then think better of going deeper into the conversation. "Nothing, never mind."

"Wait, you didn't know I was living in Bastrop? Did you?" Christian asks. I can see he is surprised that I have been kept in the dark.

I shake my head. "Last I heard, you were a drifting roadie, a different band every few months, a different town every week."

Christian glances at the floor as he responds. I can tell he's thinking about his past. "When you say it like that, it sounds like a bad country song. The ex-stripper and the washed up roadie, we would definitely be a chart topper."

I snicker. "Someone is going to hear that and actually think I was a stripper."

"Well, if the stiletto fits." He grins at me.

"Private showings I did for you don't count." *Damn it, why in the hell did I just say that?*

He raises his eyebrows as my face turns to a bright

shade of red, then says, "My days on the road were a while ago. I found a better gig."

I sigh a huge breath of relief that he moved our conversation back on track. Then, with my voice dripping with sarcasm, I comment, "I don't know, from what I heard, you were leaving a trail of broken hearts behind you. Seems like you had a pretty decent gig."

He seems amused by my statement, which doesn't surprise me in the least. "I don't know about that," he says with that crooked smile, the one I refuse to stare at. *Damn it! I'm staring at it.* Looking away, I allow my eyes to travel to his clothes. A flannel shirt with reds, browns, and creams in it hangs open, unbuttoned, with a white V-neck t-shirt peeking out underneath. His faded blue jeans hug his hips perfectly, a tear in the knee, beginning to unravel, allows his tanned flesh to show through. The way he dresses now is different than when we were young, but something is so right about it. He's less kept, with his hair longer, the stubble on his face complementing his strong jaw line. He has a confidence that's different. It feels like he's found who he is, and I can't help but wonder who that might be.

"Emmie said you started your own business," I add.

He nods, glancing out the door over his shoulder. I wonder if he's expecting someone. "I did. I make furniture, signs, well, just about anything you can make out of wood. Actually, I made that counter."

I look down and stare at the stained red wood top, the edge cascading to a waterfall point that leads the wood grain all the way to the floor. The polish and stain accentuates the knots in the woods, the simplicity in the piece is part of its beauty.

"Are you kidding?" I ask in disbelief.

"Nope, I do most of their frames here, too," he adds.

My eyes dart around the room, taking in all the variations of wood tones in front of me. My stare stops at one of Emmie's oversized paintings. It's one of my favorites called *The Breaking*. Walking up to the six foot painting, I run my hands along the frame, which looks like driftwood that has been smoothed down and sealed. The wood is so soft it's like silk under my fingertips.

"Christian, these are beautiful," I remark, moving on to the next frame, which has ornate scroll carvings to complement the realistic oil painting it surrounds.

"Thanks."

"No, I mean it! I can't believe you made all of these," I gasp.

"I have a lot of time on my hands, I guess. I mostly make furniture, now that the shop's open. I have enough custom orders to last me the next six months," he adds proudly.

I turn and look at him; he looks away, his eyes shifting nervously around the room. It's not a reaction I recall ever seeing from him, nor one I expect.

"Seriously, you're very gifted."

He clears his throat, my compliment making him uncomfortable. The Christian I knew was confident to the point of arrogance. The man that stands before me has a sense of humbleness about him. "Thanks, I enjoy it. And I get to be here and watch Olivia grow up."

"She's amazing," I say, walking over and remembering

my tea, which has now shifted to a muddy coloring. Pulling out the bag and placing it on the nearby saucer, I drop in the sugar cube that was waiting on the plate. I can't believe I'd been nervous to see Christian. It feels completely normal to be around him. There is none of the intensity or tension I'd worried about.

"Let's go to dinner," he suggests.

My body jolts; perhaps I am wrong. There is nothing normal about him asking me out to dinner. How could I be so stupid? Of course, leave it up to Christian to assume he could just charm his way back into my life, even after knowing I'm engaged to someone else. Maybe he hasn't changed that much.

"Um, yeah, so that's not going to happen," I answer, not shielding the disgust.

"Why not? We have years to catch up on."

"Because, I'm engaged or did that slip your mind?"

"Wow." Christian laughs. "I see you're also still very sure of yourself."

"Excuse me?" I bark at him.

"It's all right, I always liked your confidence." he says, waving his hands in the air defensively.

"No, that's not what I meant. I mean—well—you're the one who asked me to dinner. I don't think that means I'm full of myself."

"I asked an old friend to dinner. It's not like it is a date or something."

"Yeah right," I scoff, squinting at him, before sipping my over-steeped and bitter tea.

"Oh, now I get it," Christian says, nodding.

I furrow my brow. "Now you get what?"

"You're scared to go to dinner with me."

"What?"

"You are!" he exclaims. "You're scared it might stir some of those old feelings."

"What? You've got to be kidding me!"

"All right then, so you'll go to dinner with me? I'll pick you up tonight at eight," he adds, not waiting for me to answer before setting the time.

"No!" I gasp, unsure how the conversation slipped away from me so quickly. "I'm not sixteen anymore. I know when you're manipulating me."

Christian flashes that slightly crooked smile at me. That damn cavernous dimple of his is staring at me. I can't look away, so I just make myself look annoyed. He walks up, leaning onto the counter, so he's only inches away from me now. He smells like cedar chips, and I feel my knees begin to buckle under me. I grab the counter top to steady myself.

"No manipulation, I really just want to have dinner with one of my oldest friends. You can even talk about Henry all night if you want," he offers before standing upright.

"Fine, I just might." Yup, I sound like a moron.

"Great, see you tonight at eight," he says, spinning around and exiting the shop. The bell dings before I can say another word.

Then I'm alone, still gripping the counter, and wondering what on Earth just happened.

～

CHAPTER 8

I LOOK AT myself in the mirror, the third outfit I've tried staring back at me. The first one was far too sexy for a friends-only dinner, the second one looked like I should be painting a room in it, and now there is this one. I'm pretty sure it is stylish while still saying, 'This is not a date, so please don't get the wrong idea.' Though Christian had made it quite clear this was not a date already.

When Henry called earlier and asked what I had been up to, I considered telling him about the dinner. I then reconsidered, because, after all, it isn't a date. If it is just dinner with an old friend, then it shouldn't be that big of a deal, and why even bother telling him. At least that's how I justified it in my head.

Flattening out the ruffles on the dress, I marvel at one of my creations. It is a veritable fountain of lace and frills, from the handmade appliqué on the form-fitting bodice, to the cascading layers of chiffon cream and cocoa colored ruffles on the skirt, stopping just above the knee.

It's young and flirty without being inappropriate for the purpose of the evening. Considering I'm in Texas, I only think it proper to pair it with my favorite pair of Frye cowboy boots, which come midway up my shin. I look pretty darn adorable if I do say so myself.

"Paige," I hear with a knock at my door, my heart jumping a little. "It's me, Emmie, can I come in?"

I turn to face her as she enters. "Sure."

"Wow, I love that dress. Is that an original Paige design?"

"It is," I reply, spinning around, showing off the details.

"Oh my God, you have to make me something," Emmie begs, rushing in and rubbing the ruffles between her fingertips.

"Hey, I made your wedding dress!" I remind her.

"Trust me, I remember, it's my favorite piece of clothing I own, but I think people might begin to wonder if I'm crazy if I wear it around the shop all day."

"Artists are eccentric, right?"

"Very true, so maybe I could get away with it." We both burst out laughing and take a seat on the bed.

"So what's up?" I inquire.

"Christian told Colin to have you meet him at his studio at eight instead," Emmie says hesitantly.

"Oh … all right," I reply, trying not to make it sound like a big deal.

"Well?" she pushes. It is clear she isn't going to fold easily.

"Well what?" I continue to play dumb.

"I came back from Olivia's doctor appointment and you said nothing happened. Clearly that wasn't true."

"Oh, Christian, that's nothing," I insist.

"Nothing? You look amazing, your fiancé is in New York, and you're supposed to meet up in a few minutes with the only guy who ever broke your heart? That's not nothing."

"Emmie," I say, grasping her hands. "Really, I promise, it's nothing. If it were something, don't you think I would have told you?"

"No, I don't think you would have said a word either way. That's how you work."

I laugh. "You do know me too well. But I swear, it's nothing."

"Nope, no way—that's not going to work for me. Spill it, what's going on?"

"Honestly," I begin. "I have no clue. It all happened so fast. He came by the gallery this afternoon to deliver a package to me."

"A package, huh?" she interjects with a sly grin.

"You've been down here with the Bennett boys too long," I remark.

"Yeah, you're probably right. Go on, what happened next?"

"We got to talking and before I knew it, I 'd agreed to a friends dinner. Whatever the hell that means."

"I don't know, sweetie, do you think it's a good idea?" Emmie asks, her voice heavy with concern.

"No! I think it's a terrible idea. But before I could change my mind, he was gone. And now, if I don't show, he'll make it into a big deal, I'm sure, and say I'm not over him," I argue.

"Are you?"

"Am I what?"

"Over him?"

I look at her in shock. "Of course I am. How could you ask that? I love Henry."

"I know you do," she confirms.

"Then why do I always feel like I have to convince you of that?"

"It's not whether you love Henry that worries me. It's how much you loved Christian."

"Loved. That's in the past. I don't love him any more," I reply firmly.

"Okay," she relents. "I'm sorry. If you say you're over him, then I'm sure you are."

I stand, straightening out my dress and quickly glance in the mirror to fix my hair, but not too much as to make it look like I care. "I'll see you later."

"Have fun."

"I doubt I will," I say and head out the door and down the wooden stairwell, my boots clicking as they hit. The gallery is closed, and I have to exit out of the rear door, which is the one they use for their residence. The wood studio was only just off to the side of that.

I push open the door that has a note with a phone number printed on it advising visitors to call for an appointment. The room is lit in soft, yellowy light. Immediately, the wood smell hits me—intoxicating. The room is set up like a showroom floor. A rustic looking dining room table and chairs are front and center, and an ornate, hand-carved rocking chair is in the far corner. I even see a pair of wooden skis hanging on the wall, and I laugh, imagining someone on skis in the desert terrain.

"I'm back here," I hear Christian's voice call from an open door at the back of the room.

I walk across the pine floor, noticing all of the knotting and patterns as I move. Even the floor is a work of art.

"Oh my God," I say as I approach. "This place is amazing."

Moving into the open doorway, I see Christian standing there in just a pair of jeans and a face-mask, wood shavings sticking to his sweaty chest. He moves in long strides, rubbing the sanding block up and down on the top of the large flat surface in front of him.

"I'm sorry—" I shriek. "I thought you said eight." I turn around, my cheeks shifting to a fiery red.

"I did, but I got a call rushing an order, so I thought I'd work on it until you came over," he explains.

"Shirtless?" I can't help my snarky tone.

"I didn't want to get sawdust all over my shirt, so I thought I'd take it off until you got here. You always took forever getting ready."

As I turn around, he is rubbing a towel down his washboard abs. I swallow hard. His body has changed, his shoulders and arms are broader, but his waist is trimmer. I always liked his body, but now, with the cuts just below his hips, I can see his new physique has a lot to offer as well.

"Besides, you're engaged." I can tell he's making fun of me.

"Shut up. Do you need a few minutes?" I ask.

"To what?"

"Get dressed."

"You've seen me in a lot less than this." He laughs. Damn him, now I am thinking about him with less—he had the most amazingly firm ass. I always loved seeing him walk from our bed to the bathroom ... naked. I shake my head and tell myself to think of something else.

"Whatever. So where are we going for dinner?" I ask, trying to think quickly, careful not to look away again. I don't want him to think for a second that his undressed state makes me feel uncomfortable. If I'm being completely honest, I also don't mind looking a little longer.

He grabs a nearby white t-shirt, slipping it over his head, then pulls on the same flannel he had on that morning. Clearly, it is not a date.

"There's a great little place called Roadhouse, but it's not in walking distance, and I'm kind of in the mood to walk."

"Seriously? What is it about this Roadhouse place? The cab driver mentioned it, too." I laugh.

"It's good!"

"Can a place called Roadhouse really be that good?" I joke.

Suddenly his face shifts, and he becomes very serious. Turning, he picks something up from the chair and faces me. I watch as he places a cowboy hat on top of his head and secures it firmly into place. His glare never shifts as he says, "Why yes, Ms. New York, a place called Roadhouse can be quite delicious, and I would be careful if I were you."

A massive amount of air blows past my lips, sending

saliva flying everywhere as I cackle and ask, "Why's that? You plan to hog tie me, buck-a-roo?"

"Hey," Christian wails, pulling his hat off to stare at it, then back at me as if he is deeply wounded by my remarks.

"I'm sorry, you just look—" I'm not quite sure of the word I am looking for, though ridiculous has popped into my mind.

"Ruggedly handsome?" he suggests, placing the hat back on top of his head. "Why yes, I think so, too. And you better be careful, because the locals here, they take their food very seriously, and if any of them hear you badmouth Roadhouse, they're liable to run you out of town."

"That's it, it's settled. No walking. You're taking me to this Roadhouse, so I can see it for myself," I demand, still trying to contain my laughter from seeing him in his hat.

"Fine, truck's out back," Christian relents.

"Wait, did you say truck?"

"Look lady, when in Rome."

"Clearly." I giggle again as he walks past me.

"Get the lights on your way out," he instructs, walking over and securing the front door. I flip the switch to the back room, which surprisingly also shut off the lights to the showroom. Suddenly, I realize I am in the dark ... alone with Christian.

Lunging for the side door I had entered through, I breathe a sigh of relief as the light from the parking area bleeds into the room.

"What's with you?" he asks as he moves toward me, furrowing his brow.

"I've developed a fear of the dark," I say, trying to sound funny, but quickly realizing I sound insane.

"All right then," he huffs, coming to a stop and looking at me. I look back at what he's doing. Am I supposed to say something? "Well?" he asks.

"Well what?"

"Have you developed a fear of doorways, too?"

I laugh awkwardly and step outside, breathing in the fresh air. Yup, this night is going great so far. I wait as he locks the door behind me and leads the way to his truck.

"Now, just so you know, we have a ton of whitetail deer around here, so if you're driving at night you need to be careful."

"Thanks, Captain Safety."

"Fine, see if I try to help you anymore," he snaps, but I can tell we are still joking with one another.

"Besides, I'm not really planning to do any night driving around here, so I think we're good." I reply.

He looks back at me before opening the passenger door of the newer gray pick up truck. "Colin said you are going to be here for a couple months."

I climb into the oversized vehicle, and to my recollection, I had never set foot into such a beast. "I'm thinking about it, but I haven't decided yet," I reply through the open window after he shut the door, leaving out that he is why I am reconsidering staying.

"Oh," Christian begins before walking around and getting into the driver's side. He turns the key and, looking over at me, adds, "That's odd. He made it sound like a sure thing. He said Em was super excited about helping you plan the wedding."

"She is?" I ask, surprised by the revelation. "I wasn't sure when we talked if it was even something she wanted to do. I was afraid I was putting too much on her with the gallery and the baby."

"Are you kidding me? Em and her best friend's wedding. It's all she's been talking about since you got engaged." There is no pain in his voice. He isn't hurting over me marrying someone else. I breathe a sigh of relief as I realize, in fact, this is just a friendly dinner, and I have nothing to worry about.

Except for Em. I had been so hateful to her before I left, and all she was doing was trying to look out for me. I need to remember to do something extra nice for her when I get home.

"All right, so I gotta know," I continue. "A roadie— what were you thinking?"

Christian takes a deep breath, his eyes never shifting from where his headlights hit the road.

"I'm sorry, it's none of my business," I quickly add, sensing his hesitation.

"No, that's not it," he says. "It's just— it's embarrassing."

"Christian Bennett! I've known you since we were kids, and you've never gotten embarrassed about anything. Let me guess, you did it for a girl."

He smiles, but still says nothing.

"Oh, wait, it wasn't a girl at all, was it? I had no clue," I say, insinuating perhaps he is more interested in boys.

"Huh?"

"It's cool, and it actually explains a lot about why we didn't work out," I continue.

"What explains a lot?" he demands.

"You became a roadie because you were trying to impress a boy," I say, keeping a straight face. "And I want you to know, I completely support you. I think it's very brave of you to come out and be so open about it."

"What the hell are you talking about?" Christian gasps, looking back and forth between the road and my face. His expression is too much for me to handle. I burst out laughing, unable to contain it any longer.

"Something isn't right about you," he remarks firmly, reaffixing his gaze on the highway.

"Oh, come on." I slug him playfully in the arm. "Since when did you become so serious? If it wasn't for a girl, then why'd you leave New York?"

"I never said it wasn't for a girl."

My heart sinks. I had always assumed he left for a girl, but to have him confirm that, only a few months after I left for the European modeling job, he had already moved on, stung. I realize I'm staring at him. *Don't stare. Look anywhere but at him. Change the subject. He can't see that this hurts. Don't let him see.*

"Do you enjoy what you do now?" I ask, before forcing myself to look away.

Christian seems to be thinking about my question. "I love it. You know that I've always enjoyed working with my hands. I don't have to keep regular hours, since most of my sales are through custom orders, and when I can't sleep, I can stay up all night working if that's what I want to do."

"You still have trouble sleeping?" I ask, a little surprised he had continued to be plagued by the affliction.

When Christian's parents died, he was only ten years old. He had night terrors most of his childhood, which then manifested into insomnia as an adult. Originally, that was how his drinking problem started. The alcohol helped him sleep.

When he quit drinking he would sometimes be up for days. That was when we figured out sex was a huge help. I shiver as I think about the passionate nights we used to share, ending only when exhaustion would overcome us.

"It's gotten bad again since I stopped drinking."

"Wait, what?" The words slip from my lips, dripping with disbelief.

"You don't have to sound so surprised."

"No, it's … I didn't …" My thought trails off, and I fall silent.

He looks at me; there is a pain in his eyes. I've seen it before—long ago—when he had been vulnerable enough in his youth to tell me all of the things he felt might burst from his grieving heart. It is a vulnerability I have not seen in his adulthood.

"You didn't know," he says more as a statement than a question. "I stopped when Olivia was born."

"She's ten months old."

"I know. I'm her uncle."

"I'm sorry, it's just, well, Em and Colin never mentioned you stopped drinking again."

"I'm sure they were waiting to see if it stuck."

"Ten months is a long time. I'd say it stuck."

"That's how I actually discovered I could do this woodworking. I'd just moved here, determined to stop drinking, and prove myself to Colin and Em so they would be all right with me being a part of Olivia's life. I hadn't slept in two days, and the crazy was starting to set in. I picked up a hunk of wood in the back of the gallery, and I carved. I had no idea what I was making. I just kept going."

"So did it help you sleep?"

Christian nodded. "It did. My shoulders were sore, and I was starving, but my body gave into the fatigue, and then I slept. I got up the next day and started all over again. I worked all day. By the end of the week I had a set of hand-carved skis."

"Wait, are those the ones on your wall?" I laugh, remembering the oddity.

"I had no clue what I was making when I started. They just kind of took shape eventually. I hang them there to remind me to always move forward, never back."

The hair on my arms stands up. "Wow."

"It's just what I do, no big deal," he adds modestly, turning the wheel, pulling into a gravel parking lot. I resist the urge to lean over and hug him.

Leaning to one side and peering out the window, the now famous Roadhouse comes into view. An unassuming building with rust-colored exterior walls and a tin roof sits surrounded by parked cars. There is a deck area with picnic benches and tables that are over-flowing with locals.

"This place is hopping," I comment.

"You're going to love their portabella burger with sweet potato fries."

"No, this is Texas. I thought everything was bigger in Texas. What happened to a huge beef patty?"

"Oh no, you're right, everything is bigger in Texas. They've got the biggest damn portabellas you've ever seen."

I start laughing. As Christian gets out of the truck, a warmth falls over me. That is it, the friend I'd been missing. Not that Henry isn't my friend, as well. Christian just knows me in a way nobody else can. No matter how many stories I tell Henry about my mom and our past, Christian saw it. He lived it with me. He was there through all the issues of my youth. I suppose most of my problems were actually my mother's problems, or related to the vile men she would bring home. Christian never tried to fix it—the same as I couldn't fix his parents dying. All we could do was simply be there, together. I never thought I could have that friend back, but hope is growing in me that it might be possible.

My door creaks open, and I beam a smile at him.

"What's that goofy look for?" he quickly asks.

I shake my head. "I don't know—just having a good time."

"Now now, Paige, you're a promised woman, so don't go getting a crush on me."

"In your dreams." I hop out of the truck.

"How'd you know?" Christian laughs.

"Know what?"

"That you're running through my dreams every night," he says, cracking the widest grin.

"Yeah, and I'm the one who's not right in the head," I reply, slugging him in the arm again.

"The punching thing," Christian moans. "Why couldn't that have been the one thing you grew out of?"

"Oh," I answer thoughtfully. "I did. I just like punching you. Now can we please go eat? I'm starving."

"You got it." He leads the way to open the large glass door.

Once we are seated at our modest table and the food is ordered, Christian looks at me, and suddenly the tables are turned, he begins asking me the questions.

"So Henry, he seems like a ... a nice guy."

"Don't start," I warn, tilting my head and flashing a smile.

"What? I'm serious. He seems ... *nice.*"

"It's the way you say it, and you know it," I argue.

He snickers. "All right, I'm just playing. He was your date at Em and Colin's wedding, wasn't he?"

"I didn't think you noticed I was there."

"Why would you say that?"

"You didn't even say hello. I mean, really? I was the maid of honor, and you were the best man."

"Okay, okay, I'll admit it. I had every intention of making nice, and then you showed up with a date, and ... well, I couldn't."

"I get it, it's not easy. I was kind of relieved we didn't have to speak."

"It's not so bad now, is it?" he asks, huge puppy dog eyes staring back at me.

"No, but I think it's because we've both moved on and have other things in our lives."

Christian looks back at the kitchen, searching for any sign on the status of our food. "Henry does seem to make you happy," he adds at last.

"He really does."

"I'm happy for you. So tell me all about this guy. How did you meet, what does he do? I want all the details."

I wrinkle my forehead and ask cautiously, "Are you sure?"

"Of course, this is the kind of stuff friends talk about. I want to know everything about your new life," he insists.

And so I tell him everything. We talk all through dinner, the drive home, and then even stand in the courtyard talking. Nothing is off limits. Nothing feels weird. He isn't jealous, and he actually seems genuinely interested. I wonder if he misses our friendship as much as I do.

When a silence at last lingers, he chimes, "You better get to bed."

"Are you going to be able to sleep, or is it back to the studio for you?" I question.

"What can I say, it's my routine," he answers, walking backward as he watches me quietly sneak in through the back door of Em and Colin's home.

CHAPTER 9

I WAKE UP late, look at my phone, and realize I've missed a call from Henry. I decide he can wait, as I sit up and get a look at the clock. 9:26.

When I came upstairs, after my evening with Christian, I was suddenly troubled with a case of insomnia, something very rare for me. I'd sketched into the early morning hours.

Reaching down, I pick the pad up from the floor and flip through the pages. Examining the ideas that had flooded out of me, I'm expecting nothing usable. Much to my surprise and delight, I see design after design that I still love in the morning light. To be quite honest, they are better than anything I've ever created. I find myself loathing the designs I've already made for my show. There is cohesion in the images that I have seemingly struggled with before. I've never included a vest in any of my designs, yet here are at least three within the pages of sketches.

The words urban country pop into my head. There it

is, the entire show, the concept shifting in the blink of an eye. The beauty of the south is taking things slow, doing it right. I want to take all the textures and patterns that make you think Southern style and put them on urban lines. The cut of a nice blazer paired with the perfect blue jean. Oh crap! If I'm going to commit to this, it means starting over from scratch. I have to think on this some more; any major decisions prior to my morning coffee always leads to disaster.

Stumbling out of bed, I slip on my robe, pulling the fabric up to my nose and inhaling deeply. It still smells of home, my home with Henry. I decide I'll call him after coffee. He will be honest about the makeover idea— complete and total honesty is something I can always rely on from Henry.

Shuffling down the stairs, I weave through the halls and make my way into the rustic kitchen, the smell of muffins filling the air. Emmie is dancing with Olivia near the stove to a song on the radio I've not heard.

She spins around, dancing her way over to me. "Oh my, Ms. Olivia, look who joined us. Can you say hi to Auntie Paige?"

My heart warms as Olivia giggles and gurgles, her mom suddenly dipping her back in a dramatic dance move.

"What's gotten into you?" I ask.

"I don't know what you mean," she replies, throwing a puzzled glance in my direction.

"Dancing in the morning ... what did you do with the Emmie I know?"

"Tell Aunt Paige that just because she's a grumpy puss,

and her date must have went terrible, she doesn't need to bring us all down," Emmie says in a baby-like tone.

My stomach twists and suddenly my face flashes with heat. My reaction is pure instinct. "How about you tell your mommy to hush it when she doesn't know what the hell she's talking about."

"Whoa!" Emmie replies quickly. "I was just kidding. No reason to get nasty."

I sit silently, avoiding eye contact, unsure why what she said bothered me so intensely.

"I'm serious," Emmie continues. "I didn't mean anything by it. Did something happen?"

"What?" I snap. "What does that mean?"

"I don't know." She grabs a mug and pours me a cup of coffee without asking. "Clearly something has you on edge."

"I'm fine, but I just don't like the jokes about Christian and me."

"All right, I'm sorry."

I feel bad and wish I hadn't reacted so swiftly. "Since when do you bake?" I ask, shifting the attention away from my behavior.

"There are a lot of things I started doing since we moved down here," Emmie says. "I know you're all Manhattan girl, but I think this town will really start growing on you."

"I think it already has," I say, remembering the recent inspiration in my designs.

"What? My ears must be deceiving me."

"You're not the only one who has changed," I say with a smile, scooping the sugar into my black coffee.

"Oh, do tell." Emmie plops a muffin on the table in front of me, no concern for a plate or napkin underneath it. I smile, thinking of Henry's pet peeve. Pulling up a chair, she sits down, bouncing Olivia on her knee.

"Tell what?"

"All these things that have changed about you. I feel like we never get to talk these days, and when we find time to Skype, it's always baby stuff."

"Seriously?" I gasp. "You can't just put me on the spot like that. It's not like I can just list things off."

"Today is Colin's morning for the gallery, so please, let's talk about something," Emmie pleads, grabbing my arm. "What about last night?"

"What about it?" I reply quickly.

"You went out with Christian, right?"

"Yeah, so?"

"So, tell me, how did it go?" she pushes.

"You do realize I'm engaged to be married," I remind her.

She glares at me. "Um, I know. I'm not accusing you of —" She pauses to place her hands over Olivia's ears before whispering, "screwing him."

I laugh. Screwing has somehow become a curse word since Emmie became a mother. It is actually quite endearing, and I want to squeeze my friend to pieces.

"He took me to dinner, then we came home, and I went to bed," I say at last.

"Oh no, that won't do at all," Emmie protests. "Where did you go to dinner?"

Picking up the muffin, I take a sniff, trying to identify

what is inside. There is a hint of banana and cinnamon. "You made these?" I ask nervously.

"Yes, and they're good."

"Do you have the number for poison control handy?"

"Shut up! They're good." Emmie slaps my arm playfully. "Quit changing the subject and tell me about last night."

Lifting the delicious-smelling muffin up to my lips, I take a huge bite, allowing the moist mixture to dissolve in my mouth.

With a swallow, I take a sip of the coffee in front of me, then moan in delight. "Oh my God, that is crazy good!"

"Told you."

"I'm going to get so fat by my wedding."

"Somehow I doubt that. Now spill it. Where did you go to dinner last night?"

"Why do you want to know so bad?" I ask, delighting in her torture at this point.

"I don't have a ton of girlfriends I get to dish with down here. Can't you throw me a bone or something? I mean Jesus, it's spit up and dirty diapers all day long. I could—" She's getting heated.

"All right, all right, I'm just messing with you. Careful before you start lactating. He took me to Roadhouse."

"Mmm …" Emmie moans. "I love their portabella burger."

"That's what I got! And dear God, those sweet potato fries? That place just isn't right," I say. "And I go back to my original statement that I am going to be so fat by the wedding."

I see Emmie flinch, and then realize my use of curse words in front of Olivia. "Sorry."

"Was it weird?" Emmie continues, ignoring my apology.

I think about her question for a minute. "Honestly, no. It was like old times—well, not exactly like old times."

"So you only went to dinner?"

"Yeah, we ended up staying until they closed. He was really curious about Henry, and when I talked about him he didn't get weird at all. I would have never thought we could be friends again, but apparently it's possible."

"Did he talk about you guys at all?"

"Not really. It was more catching up on what's happened over the past four years. I was glad to hear he seems to have conquered the drinking again." Then, before I thought about it I ask, "Why wouldn't you have told me?"

"Huh?" Emmie grunts in confusion.

"Why didn't you tell me he'd stopped drinking? He seems to really have his crap together." I wince, the curse word slipping past my lips again.

But this time Emmie doesn't seem upset, as she is focusing on my question. "Why would I have told you?"

"Because it's Christian," I answer quickly, slightly annoyed she would think I wouldn't care.

"You were moving in with Henry when Christian came back."

"So ..." I still don't understand her reasoning.

"The best way for a new relationship to work is to leave old ones in the past." Emmie's words feel sharp, and my defenses go up.

"I still care for him. I can't believe you'd think I wouldn't want to know. I'm a little hurt."

"Are you sure that's why you're upset?"

"What's that supposed to mean?" I demand, pushing my mug away and fixing my eyes on Emmie's face.

"Why are you flipping out on me?" Emmie asks, increasing the pace at which she is bouncing Olivia on her knee.

"I'm not flipping out," I correct her, making sure my tone was in check. "I just don't get why you would think I wouldn't want to know that Christian got his life back on track. We were together since we were kids. Just because we're not together anymore, doesn't mean I don't care."

"Look, Ashton haunted my relationship with Colin for the longest time. I just didn't want you to have the same baggage with Henry," Emmie explains, her voice shaking. Even though the conversation is clearly upsetting her, I am too angry to care.

"Christian wasn't my husband, and he wasn't a bastard who killed himself!" I snarl, without thinking my words through.

"No, but he was someone you still loved when you broke up. And just because I wanted to leave Ashton when he killed himself, didn't mean I didn't still love him when he—" She stops herself. "Forget it. I guess I should have told you."

"I don't have feelings for Christian." I'm not sure if I'm telling Emmie or myself.

"Good."

"I love Henry, and we're going to get married," I add.

"I'm glad."

81

Suddenly, my phone begins to vibrate in the pocket of my robe. Pulling it out, I see Henry's face smiling at me. "See," I say, flashing her the phone. "I love him so much, I'm going to tell him about my evening, and he won't even care."

Pushing away from the table, I wish I could rewind and redo the entire end of our conversation. Even though I know I looked like a complete and`raving lunatic, I just keep going. Walking up the stairs, I swipe the bar on my phone, clearing my throat. "Hello baby."

"There she is," Henry says softly. "God, I miss you."

"I miss you, too."

"Have you gotten work done?" Henry asks, and the complete show makeover immediately returns to my mind. I tell him everything, describing each sketch in great detail. He loves the concept, confirming the insane idea that I will have to start over.

We talk for at least an hour, discussing plans for the wedding, as well as all the things I'm missing in New York. His grandmother apparently isn't happy with us. Not surprisingly, she wanted to be much more involved in the planning, and with me in Texas it is making it next to impossible for her. Toward the end of the call a silence lingers between us, neither wanting to hang up with the other one.

"So anything else going on down there?" he asks me.

A lump grows in my throat. I need to tell him. Christian is only a friend, and by keeping it from Henry I'm making it into something else. I am making it into something wrong and something that has me snapping at my friends.

"Actually, I wanted to talk to you."

"Uh-oh." Henry laughs.

"What?"

"You're making me nervous. You're not breaking up with me are you?"

"Yup, you've got me. I secretly wanted to come to Texas and manipulated you into sending me here, so I could break up with you over the phone. Excellent plan, huh?"

"I knew it!" he exclaims. "But that's okay."

"What?" I gasp.

"I was manipulating you at the same time. I wanted you to go to Texas so I could hit on all your model friends while you were gone."

I start laughing so hard I have to clutch my side.

"What?" he moans. "Is it that hard to believe I could be a player."

"Yes," I answer. "And I know you hate my friends."

"I don't hate them, I just—" Henry pauses—probably trying to think of how to best describe his feelings. "Don't like them.

"Oh, shut up you big dork," I say.

"Sorry, but seriously, what's with the ominous statement? We need to talk? Is everything all right?"

"Oh yeah, everything's great. But something happened, and I just think you should know."

The line is silent except for his breathing.

"Henry?" I ask, ensuring he can still hear me.

"I'm here. Just dying to know what this thing is I should know."

"It's really not a big deal," I reassure him, wishing I had approached the subject shift differently.

"So … what's up?" he asks.

"I found out Christian lives here now," I say plainly. I close my eyes and hold my breath as I wait for his response.

"With Colin and Emmie?" he inquires, the revelation confusing him.

"Oh no, he lives in his own place next door," I explain, quickly continuing, deciding I need to alleviate any concern he might have. "I didn't know he was here when I decided to come. And honestly, it's not even that big a deal. I saw him last night, and we talked, and most of his questions were about us. He said he wants to be friends and even told me he was happy for us."

I wait. Hoping. Not sure what for. I just want to hear something. Something that tells me I'm not wrong about it not being a big deal. As the silence grows I begin to doubt my choice. Maybe I should have turned around and gotten on a plane as soon as I saw Christian was here. Have I betrayed Henry?

"Okay," he says, at last.

"Okay?"

"Yeah, if you say it's nothing, I trust you."

"You're not upset? I can come home if you want me to."

"Paige, stop," Henry says in a gentle voice. "I love you. We're getting married. Christian is part of who you were, not who you are. I'm not worried."

"I love you, Henry Wallace."

"And I you, Ms. Parker. Mmm …" he moans.

"What?"

"I'm so excited to make you Mrs. Paige Wallace," he answers.

My heart aches. He's the perfect other half for me. Contentment comes with him in a way I haven't known in my life before.

"Same here."

"You're excited to make me Mrs. Paige Wallace?"

"Shut, up, you know what I mean."

I listen to Henry's laugh and smile to myself.

"All right beautiful, you have an entire collection to re-work."

"Oh God, don't remind me."

"I'll talk to you tomorrow?"

"You better."

"Love you."

"Love you, too."

And then I hear the line click. Henry is right; I need to get to work, but first, I need to tell one of the greatest friends a girl could have that I'm sorry.

∾

CHAPTER 10

*I*T'S AMAZING HOW quickly one can fall into a routine. It's been nearly a month, and it seems like this day-to-day existence has been my norm for years. I wake up and have breakfast with the Bennetts. Apparently Christian has breakfast with them every morning, but initially kept his distance in order to make sure I was comfortable.

Once I told Henry about Christian being there, any discomfort I had been feeling, disappeared. There was no longer a secret, no longer a reason I should feel like I was betraying my fiancé. I shared my talk with Henry with Emmie, but she didn't have much to say, and the subject hasn't seemed to come up again.

Christian still knows how to make everyone laugh. One morning he came in dressed in one-piece, red long underwear, and a pair of cowboy boots. His broad shoulders and lean muscular physique were accentuated in the get up, but even his sexiness couldn't keep me from busting out in a full belly laugh.

He acted like he couldn't figure out what was so funny. Even Olivia had joined in on the giggle-fest. He played up the antics perfectly, causing squeals to pour from the little girl.

I can only imagine the excitement Emmie must have in her life with the Bennett boys back together. Only yesterday Christian snuck over, adding a healthy dose of pepper to Colin's eggs. He waited for his brother to dig in. Frustrated when Colin ate everything but the tampered-with eggs, he scooped up a heap of his own eggs and shoved them into his mouth, and then proceeded to spit them out across the room when he discovered Colin had already coated his eggs with a massive amount of salt.

Emmie always pretends to be annoyed, but it is clear she has fallen right into place in her role as Mrs. Bennett. I'm happy for her. The walls she had up when I first met her seem to be completely demolished. This is her family, and it is clear they can't live without her. I think part of me envies her. I'm not sure exactly why, but there is a familiarity in being back with boys. I know my life is with Henry, and soon we will be starting our own story, but I can't help feeling like sometimes she stole my identity. I feel terrible for even thinking it.

Once breakfast is over I will spend my morning either sketching or sewing. Tossing out the old drawings and starting from scratch has been the best decision I could have made. Now that I am beginning to see the results there is no doubt in my mind. The ideas are just blowing out of me, sometimes faster than I can record them. All one has to do is look around this sleepy little town to see the effect it's had on everything from the color palette to the textures of fabric I've used.

My work is busting out of the small room I'm staying in. There are stacks of fabric choices all over the kitchen and stock room. I have even taken to storing some of the boxes of supplies in Christian's back room, which is less than ideal with all of the wood shaving that happens in there.

Once my work filled mornings are done, I help Emmie out in the gallery so that she can make everyone lunch. She spends her mornings painting and her afternoons running the gallery, switching off with Colin who takes care of the massive online orders in the afternoon. We've become a well-oiled machine. In the afternoon I manage to squeeze in some more work time before we all knock off early for the evening.

Every night seems to hold a new surprise. A gathering in the town park, dinner at a neighbors, or even neighbors coming over to their house. Everything is so yummy that I have to continually remind myself that I have a wedding dress to fit into.

"What are you up to today?" I hear Christian's voice over my shoulder.

I don't turn to look at him; instead, I continue my work with my seam ripper, removing my latest sewing blunder. "What I'm always up to—work."

He sits across from me at the dining table, watching me. I glance up self-consciously. "Is there something I can help you with?"

"You work too much," he states with a furrowed brow.

I shake my head then return to the ripping. "Gee, thanks for the observation."

"No, I just mean that you've been working your ass off since you got here. How about you have a little fun," Christian suggests.

"I've been having fun," I insist.

"I mean more than the Grandma/Grandpa nights Em and Colin plan for you," he argues, reaching out and placing his hand over my work, gaining my full attention. "Let's go have some fun."

"Like what?" I stare at him suspiciously.

"I don't know, we used to go all day without ever making plans—just seeing where the day would take us."

I smile as I remember the carefree times of my youth, then shake my head as the reality of the impending deadline jolts me back to reality. "I can't, I have too much to do."

He takes the shirt I was working on out of my hands and stands up. "Come on, would it kill you to have a little fun?"

He extends a hand, and I feel my heart start beating hard and fast in my chest. *What's this big deal? It's just one day. I could use the break.*

I jump to my feet and exclaim, "Let's do it! Are jeans and a t-shirt okay?"

"I hope so, because I'm not changing," Christian says as he tosses the shirt I'd been working on onto the dining room table and drags me out the back door.

"Wait, shouldn't we tell Em where we're going?" I ask with concern.

"Why, do you need permission?" He laughs.

In an instant, the adrenaline kicks in, and I suddenly feel alive. I've been going through the motions all month long, surrendering to the routine, and not realizing it is starting to suffocate me. "Hell no, let's go."

A few seconds later and we are in the truck, speeding out of the gravel lot.

"So where do you want to go?" he asks me.

"I have no idea, I assumed you had some sort of a plan."

"Because I've always been the guy with a plan, huh?"

"Point taken," I acknowledge his sarcasm. "So what is there to do around here?"

"How do you feel about a road trip?" he questions, looking at me, his smile revealing his dimple.

"How far are we talking?" I'm suddenly worried about what I have agreed to.

"You okay if we head into the city?"

"Austin?"

"Unless you know of another city I don't know about," he fires back.

"You really are charming, aren't you?" I grumble.

"That's what everyone keeps telling me." He smiles slyly.

We make small talk on the drive. He keeps asking me questions about Henry's upcoming visit. I'm not sure, at first, why he is so curious, but then decide to leave it alone. As we near the city limits I wonder if he has figured out a plan for this late afternoon."

"Okay, obviously we're headed somewhere, so where are you taking me?"

"I remembered you loved to dance. Do you still go out

dancing a lot?" He answers my question with a question of his own.

"Henry isn't really into the scene, but I'll go with my girlfriends sometimes," I answer, then realize the answer was in his question. "Wait, we're going dancing? What kind of club is open in the middle of the day?"

He squints his eyes as he thinks about my question. "Well, I'm not really sure if I would call it a club."

I shake my head. "I don't think I like the sound of this."

Christian laughs. "What, don't you trust me?"

"Not in the least," I huff, glaring at him suspiciously.

"Ouch, that hurts, it really hurts."

"Yeah, I'm sure. Spill it, where are we going?"

Before he answers, I watch as he pulls onto the exit. I look around for some sign of where we might be headed, when I see a sign that reads Congress Avenue.

"All I ask is you try it, and if you have a horrible time, we'll go do something else," Christian offers.

I laugh. "In my experience, when someone offers a disclaimer like that, it usually means I'm going to have a horrible time."

The truck pulls to one side, and with a hard bump as we hit part of the curb, I see the sign for the business where we parked. "The Two Step," I read out loud.

He pulls into an open spot and after placing the truck in park and looks over at me with a devilish grin. "I know what you're thinking," he says.

"I doubt that."

"I was the same way when I first tried it, but it's a lot of fun, I promise." I stare at him, eyebrows high on my forehead. "Come on, worst case, they have killer mozzarella sticks."

"Of course they do," I grumble as I push open the heavy door and make my way out of the truck.

"When did you become such a stick in the mud?" he asks me, and I find the words sting a little.

"I'm not a stick in the mud," I insist.

"We'll see," he taunts, opening the wooden door to the establishment. It doesn't matter that I know he's manipulating me, it's still working.

I look around the place that has a dance floor with a two-story ceiling. Everything is wood, and not in a good way—from the floors to the walls, to the tables and chairs, and let's not forget the wagon wheel light fixtures hanging from the ceiling.

"What do you think?" he asks.

"All this place needs is a big wooden Indian in the corner, and it would be one for the record books," I joke.

"There's one in the back hallway by the bathrooms."

"Of course there is, how silly of me," I mutter.

We make our way across the main seating area to the bar, where Christian orders us a couple of diet cokes and asks if we can get some mozzarella sticks. The bartender informs us the kitchen is closed until five, but he's happy to get us the diet cokes. When he walks away I say, "I thought you were kidding."

"About what?"

"The cheese sticks."

"Oh," he begins, "Heck no. I guess we'll have to order some when the kitchen opens."

I sit on the cowhide barstool, another first in my life,

and watch the various couples on the dance floor. The size of the crowd surprises me, considering it's only a quarter past four.

"Did you bring me here to do some line dancing?" I can't stop myself from laughing as I jokingly ask.

Christian doesn't answer me right away. He stands, taking a swig of his soda, before slamming it on the counter and grabbing my hand to pull me to the dance floor. "Ever done the two step?"

"No, and I can't say I've ever wanted to," I yell, as he drags me behind him effortlessly.

We pause at the edge of the dance floor, waiting for the song to end. "What are we doing?" I whisper.

"Wait for it," he instructs me.

I watch as other couples begin to gather around the edges. The room falls silent, and the crowd emerges onto the floor. Christian steps out onto the wooden arena and, with a flick of his wrist, he pushes me away from his body and then pulls me back in, my back pressed up against his chest.

A lump forms in my throat, and I swallow hard, surprised by the suddenness of his moves. A shiver runs down my spine as I feel his strong arms wrap around my waist, his hot breath on my cheek.

"I don't know if this is such a good idea," I moan, secretly not wanting him to stop.

"Just have fun with it," he whispers in my ear, and I feel my knees buckle for an instant.

I hear the woman at the microphone give a loud scream, trying to pull everyone's attention in. She proceeds to announce the dance style and exactly how everything is going to work, but she is speaking so fast I barely understand what she says.

"I don't know what I'm doing," I protest, starting to feel anxious about my foreign surroundings.

"You'll be fine, just watch what everyone else does and go with the flow." His advice does not bring me any comfort.

Before I can think, the music begins, and we are off. Christian escorts me from one side of the dance floor to the other. In one second my backside is pressed up against him, and in the next I spin around and am handed off to the next man.

I feel my head begin to swirl and my heart pound as I jump across the floor. Christian is right; I only step on a couple sets of toes before I fall into the rhythm of the movements. It is invigorating. I haven't felt so alive since ... well, for as long as I can remember. Each gentleman I dance with seems more chivalrous than the last, with Christian occasionally working back into my partner rotation.

When the song finally comes to an end, I find myself panting, but better than that, laughing. Laughing so hard it hurts.

"Are you having fun?" Christian asks, his arms wrapped around me for support.

"Are you kidding?" I gasp between breaths. "That was a blast."

"I told you," he exclaims. "Now what, you want to ride the mechanical bull?"

I burst out laughing, shaking my head. "No, I think I'll stick to dancing." Just as the words leave my lips the next song comes on—a slow song. I sigh, the pure joy of the moment shifting to awkwardness.

Christian doesn't miss a beat. His hands link behind my lower back as he pulls me in close. Instinctively, I lift my arms and wrap them around his neck. We begin swaying mindlessly to the music. I'm careful not to look into his eyes, but standing so closely, it is difficult.

"I'm really glad to see you having so much fun," he says.

I blush. *Why am I blushing? Damn it.* "Thanks for getting me out of the house."

One of my hands slips from behind his neck, and instead grips his arm. I can feel his fingers playing with the waistband of my jeans, flicking the fabric back and forth. Even though I don't want to, I find myself looking up into his eyes, searching for some idea of what he might be thinking.

He's already staring down at me, and in an instant, our eyes lock. I don't notice when we stop swaying; we're just standing on the dance floor, looking at each other.

"Are you all right?" he whispers.

I lick my lips, swallow, and nod my head yes. He presses himself against me, and I feel him trailing his fingertips across the top of my panties. I know I should push him away, but I can't.

"Are you sure?" he asks again. I know what he's actually asking me. He wants permission to go further. *Why aren't I pushing him away?* The pull between us is growing stronger with the intensity in his eyes.

I close my eyes and force myself to turn around; I need to walk away from him before I lose all control. Before I can take a step, I feel his arms wrap around me from behind and pull me back in, his hot breath blowing into my ear as he speaks deeply, "The song's not over."

His lips graze my ear, but rather than move them away, he lets them linger, touching my flesh ever so slightly. I can feel a stirring from within my body, and it's alarming, to say the least.

"I'm so glad you decided to come for a visit," he says, our bodies backed up against one another, once again swaying to the twang of the love song.

"Is it hot in here?" I ask, desperate to change the subject. "I think it's hot in here. We should get out of here."

I can feel his lips shift into a smile against the tip of me ear. The song finally slows and then falls into complete silence. His arms are still around me as I wait for him to move first. He doesn't.

Lifting my hands, I break his grasp and rush off the dance floor. I can hear him calling after me, but I don't stop. I walk as fast I can, straight out the front door, gasping for air, swallowing as much of the freshness as I can.

"Paige!" Christian yells as he emerges from the door behind me. "Will you stop? What is going on with you?"

I can feel myself trembling. I turn around and stare at him, my eyes full and wet, and lifting a finger, I point at the door and ask, "What in the hell was that?"

He doesn't look away; he's watching me, and I feel my chest begin to constrict again. He walks forward, moving in close. "What do you want it to be?"

I shake my head. "I can't do this," I protest, wiping a tear from my eye before it falls, my voice cracking.

He steps back, looking toward his truck, then down the other direction of the road. "Do you want to go for a walk?"

"What?" I ask, confusion consuming me.

"Clearly we both need a breather. Let's take a walk, and I promise I'll keep my hands in my pockets." I know he's joking, but in the back of my mind I'm thinking that might be a good idea.

I want to be back in the safety of my little room at Emmie's, but in this exact moment, the thought of getting back in the small, close quarters of the pickup truck's cab does not seem wise. "Walk where?"

He thinks for a second. "Actually, I have a really great treat for you."

Looking at him, I force a smile and nod in agreement.

"We have a little bit of a wait, but about a half-mile down this road is Congress Avenue Bridge. At sunset, a ton of people gather on the bridge to watch the bats fly out," he explains.

"Bats?" I ask cautiously.

"Trust me, it's breathtaking. I don't think I'll ever get tired of seeing that whirlwind of creatures flying up into the orange sky.

We walk to that bridge, and we watch those bats. Thankfully what happened on the dance floor doesn't come up again.

~

CHAPTER 11

*T*HANKSGIVING IS ALMOST here, and though I'm looking forward to a break, what I'm looking forward to the most is seeing my sweet Henry. Christian even seems excited to officially meet him. I thought after what happened on the dance floor he would start acting weird, but he seems to be fine.

"Emmie, can I borrow the truck?" I call into the gallery. Silence. I add, "I need to pick Henry up from the airport."

"Sure thing, hon, the keys are—"

"On the hook, I know." Without a moment's hesitation I slip the keys off the hook and am out the back door, patting my pockets to ensure I have my phone and wallet.

"Hey, where you headed all dolled up?" Christian yells from the courtyard, using the back of his arm to wipe away the sweat from his brow.

In my lifetime, I've seen Christian naked more times than I can possibly count. I have been in Texas for a month now, and have seen his muscles glistening with sweat but still, a lump always forms in my throat when I see him in such a state. I tell myself, it's a natural reaction, it doesn't mean anything. I mean, really, with those jeans he wears, it's like his body's begging to be noticed. He's an attractive guy, but so is Henry. Why am I even thinking about this? Because of that damn night at the dance club, that's why. I can't quit thinking about his. His breath on my cheek, his lips on the tip of my ear. He's acting like nothing happened, and I wonder how he does it.

I glance down at my outfit. I don't think I would exactly call myself dolled up, but I do want to impress Henry when he sees me for the time in over a month. Based on Christian's words, I am guessing I picked the right outfit.

The little summer dress is not one of my own creations. It's a rarity for me to wear something I haven't made. I can't believe it's November, and I'm wearing a summer dress. Of course I've paired it with the cutest cardigan with iron-on patches of blue birds near the top button and knee-high boots. I do look cute, and I know it. The green in the dress even makes my eyes pop.

"I'm picking up Henry from the airport," I holler back, not wanting to linger while Christian is in his current super-hot, sweaty, sexy state.

"Oh yeah, I forgot that was today."

"How could you forget? It's all I've been talking about for the past couple days." I laugh.

"All right, I confess. I didn't forget. I just didn't know what else to say," he says with a smile.

I pause for a moment, wondering what that means. *Is he trying to tell me something without actually saying it?* I shake my head and continue walking; I need to quit reading into things.

"Something's not right with you," I reply, pulling open the door of the ancient truck and stepping up inside, the door creaking loudly as I do. I'd have loved to take the Prius, but I know they need to keep that in case they have to run somewhere with Olivia.

"That's what you keep telling me. Have fun."

"Oh, I plan on it!" I exclaim, pulling the door closed behind me. I watch Christian's face contort. What the hell did that mean? Why did I say that? It sounds like I'm going to strip down in the airport parking lot and have my way with Henry. Of course, let's be real. It has been a month since I've seen him. There's a very good chance that this may happen. But still ... to say that to Christian? I must seem like such a slut.

Just drive, I tell myself. The last thing I want to do is be late when Henry gets off that plane. I throw the truck in reverse, carefully maneuver around Christian's truck, my thoughts briefly shifting to the fact that two of my friends now own trucks, and though their businesses require it of them, it still feels very odd. Pulling onto the old road behind the shops, which parallels Main Street, gravel sprays out behind the tires.

For the first ten minutes on the road I keep thinking about the comment I made to Christian. I need to quit thinking about it. I flip on the radio but am unable to get a station on the ancient device. Finally, I give up and play music on my phone, dropping it in the hollowed compartment next to the door handle.

Singing at the top of my lungs, I enjoy song after song

—Adele crooning her woes, then R.E.M. groaning about the world coming to an end. My heart skips a beat and a lump forms in my throat when the next song comes on. "Only In Dreams" by Weezer. I glance down at the tattoo on my wrist, staring at the words, 'I just might take the chance.' The memories of that night come flooding back.

When Christian and I first split, I used to listen to this song over and over, crying myself to sleep. I soon figured out that not listening to it at all was best. I thought of his match to my tattoo on his wrist that read, 'She's in my bones.' We were twenty and at a music festival. We were young, in love, with the rest of our lives ahead of us. At the time we thought there could never be another for either of us. After all, we'd been together since our mid-teen years. We'd seen it all. Together we endured the death of his parents, the destruction of my family life, and any hope of reconciliation with my mother. We were in a place where we trusted each other completely.

I was so naive. Weezer came on, the crowd was electric, and the energy swept us up. After the encore, we didn't want the night to end. Our friends went out drinking, we knew that wasn't a good thing for Christian. We walked around, under the stars, quoting the lyrics from our favorite songs to one another. I don't remember whose idea it was first, but once the idea was out, there was no stopping either of us.

The tattoo guy told us it was a good idea that we were tattooing lyrics instead of names, because when we broke up, it wouldn't be something that was hard to explain to your next partner. Christian proudly told him it didn't matter because he was going to marry me one day. There would never be a need for such an explanation. He was naïve as well.

As the song comes to an end, I see the airport exit coming up on my right, and with a quick glance over my shoulder I swerve across two lanes, narrowly catching the exit. With a deep inhale, I tell myself to put Christian out of my mind. I love Henry, and Christian is just a friend, I think.

I weave my way through the lanes of traffic and make my way into the airport parking lot. Driving the truck is completely foreign to me; I might as well be driving a tanker. I park at the end of a row with empty spots all around me. I don't trust myself to park next to another vehicle.

I jump from the truck, slam the creaky door, and head for the entrance. My heart begins to race. I'm about to see Henry; I'm so excited I can hardly stand it. I want to hold his hands in mine, kiss his tender lips, and feel him pull me close with his masculine grip. Damn it! Being away from the man you love for a month can really make a girl horny.

The sign says his flight is slightly delayed. I pace at the gate. I've been looking forward to this moment so intensely. With Christian's hard body in front of me day in and day out, it's hard to keep focus on my fiancé. I need to hold him, look at him, feel him, and that will put all those other thoughts, which I didn't want racing through my mind, to rest.

Finally, his plane lands, and though it feels like the disembarking process takes five years, he is here, walking off the plane, and smiling at me. His eyes have dark circles around them, and I can see he's clearly exhausted, but he still has a smile for me. Running across the waiting area as fast as I can, I leap into his arms. He sees me coming and doesn't hesitate, dropping his carryon and bracing for my approach.

"Paige," he cries, and then wraps his arms around me, moaning softly. A sensation of home fills me. Almost instantly, though, I feel the change in his body. Pulling away from him, I examine him closely, squeezing his side.

"You're so thin."

"I guess I miss your cooking," Henry answers with a smile, shifting uncomfortably.

"No," I continue. "This is more than that, plus we both know I can't cook at all."

"You're learning," he defends me chivalrously.

"I'm serious. What's going on?"

He shakes his head. "I've lost a little weight. It's not that big a deal."

"Please, tell me what's going on," I plead pointedly.

"It's these headaches. They've gotten so bad I don't have much of an appetite."

"I thought you were going to go to the doctor?" I press, my heart heavy with concern.

"As promised, I did," he says, raising a hand in defense. "The doctor thought maybe it was lack of rest and stress, so he tried prescribing a few things, but they didn't really work. Now he's saying it could be an allergy to something, so I go in next week for some allergy tests."

"You poor baby," I say, squeezing his somewhat unfamiliar frame close to me.

"I'll be fine. Doctor Abbott will figure this out," Henry

says with a smile, and I feel his lips press against the top of my head.

"I missed you," I say instinctively.

"I missed you, too. I love you, baby," Henry adds, never letting go of me as he picks up his bag with his free hand. "You look beautiful, by the way."

"Thanks," I say softly, my smile hidden in the side of his chest.

Reaching down and placing his fingertips under my chin, he lifts my face until my eyes are staring into his. I'm no longer looking at the dark circles or noticing the exhaustion. We are so close at this point; all I can do is get lost in the blue. As his lips come in, grazing mine, I close my eyes, drinking in every moment of the kiss. As I feel a flutter in my stomach all the passionate moments we've shared come flooding back, and I want to rip his clothes off immediately. I wish intensely we weren't in public. I moan my frustration into his mouth.

"What is it, darling?"

"I just missed you so much."

"Really?" Henry asks, and then leans close to my ear, his hot breath tickling it. "Because I've missed screwing you."

The second the dirty word is breathed into my ear, I feel my legs go weak. This man! He knows exactly how to turn me into a pile of goo.

"Oh hell," I blurt out, realizing the logistics of this kind of sucked.

"You don't like the idea of me screwing you?" He asks, confused.

"Oh no!" I exclaim. "I very much like that idea. It's just,

well … I'm in the guest room of my friends' house. Not exactly the best place to get our freak on."

"Well then, you'll be happy to know I've booked a room at the inn."

"What?"

"I didn't want to impose on your friends any further, so I booked a room before I left."

"Oh Henry, I could not love you any more right now." I squeal.

Even though Henry and I have been apart for an entire month there is no awkwardness. We fall right back into our roles, exchanging jokes and laughing, a loving couple, sure in who they are. He finds it particularly entertaining that I'm driving around in what he calls a monster truck. I kind of pride myself on the fact that he seems just a little more city than me now.

There isn't a moment of silence on the drive back. Of course, this is mostly due to the fact that I can't seem to shut up. I want Henry to know everything, well, almost everything. We talked on the phone every night, so most of what I tell him is things he already knows. Henry just watches me, jabbering on, smiling, and content to just listen.

Pulling into the vacant parking space in front of the inn, I glance down the street to see if perhaps Emmie or Colin is outside. I don't see anyone, but I can hear the sound of Christian shaving away in the courtyard.

Hopping out of the truck, I walk around next to Henry. "Should we go say hi to everyone or check in first?"

Henry looks at me with a sly grin.

"What?" I ask innocently, even though I already know exactly what that sinister look means.

"I know what I want to do."

"Henry, what about everyone else?"

"I haven't seen my fiancé in a month. Sorry if I don't give a damn about them right now," he explains, pulling me close. I feel nervous for a moment, like someone is watching us, but with his strong arms wrapped around me that feeling melts away. "I want you so bad."

"Okay," I say with a soft giggle. "Let's go."

He leans in, kissing me. You would have thought we've been apart for a year from the intense passion. He pulls away, and before I can catch my breath, he turns, pulling me up the stairs of the quaint inn in record time.

CHAPTER 12

*P*ULLING ON MY cardigan, I stare at myself in the mirror. It's quite evident from my tousled hair what has just transpired between Henry and me. Glancing around the room, I suddenly realize I hadn't paid any attention to the decor when we entered. My mind was clearly in other places.

The bed is covered in a grandma-style floral quilt, and the drapes on the windows look like they were hung thirty years ago, the lace at the edges now yellowed with age. Besides the dated feel, the room is clean, but I can't help feeling we somehow violated the room.

"Are you sure you want to stay here and not over at Colin and Em's?" I ask. I'm now quite used to my little room with the short ceilings in my friends' home. The idea of staying in these foreign surroundings for the next few days does not seem appealing.

"No, this place is fine. After all, here I won't have to worry about how loud we get," Henry replies with a devilish grin. I'm not so sure I agree with him. I can only imagine who might have their ear up against the wall in the room next to us.

"So, how do I look?" Henry asks, holding out his arms and doing a turn for me, as if he were on the runway.

"What?" I laugh, surprised by the question.

"Hey! These are your friends; I want to make a good impression. I doubt they even remember me from the wedding." My heart grows warm, the sweetness of his gesture washing over me.

"They're going to love you no matter what you're wearing," I reassure.

"Well, of course they are. I'm quite lovable, as you well know."

I walk over to him, slipping my hand between his button-up gray shirt and navy blazer. I pull his body close to me, resting my forehead on his chin. "That you are," I whisper.

"Ready?" he asks. Suddenly I feel a rush of butterflies. I'm nervous. Why am I nervous? I've talked so much about Henry it is like Colin and Emmie already know him. There is no reason to be nervous. Unless … it isn't Colin and Emmie I'm worried about at all. How will Christian act when he's actually face to face with Henry? It is very clear—by that night on the dance floor—that Christian is still feeling something for me, no matter how well he is able to hide it.

What if he's rude to Henry? How will Henry react to that? What if Henry starts to suspect something is going on between us? There's nothing going on! I want to scream the words, but know that would prove very confusing for Henry.

"Babe?" Henry questions, his voice vibrating through my forehead. "Are you all right?"

"Of course," I say, pulling away and flashing him a smile. "Let's head over. It's almost dinner time, and I'm famished."

"Yeah, you need some good, Texan food to fatten you up for the wedding."

I take hold of Henry's hand to lead him from the room. He pulls away, to turn and walk over to his overnight bag, removing a small bottle from the pouch on the side.

"What are you doing?" I inquire.

"Oh, nothing, just something the doctor gave me to help with the headaches," Henry explains.

"Are they that bad?" I ask, staring at him sympathetically.

"No, not all the time. You're not reconsidering are you?"

"What are you talking about?" I'm confused.

"Marrying me. Are you thinking about trading in your nerdy allergy-ridden fiancé? You know the vows specifically say 'in sickness and in health.'"

"Hmm …" I begin, pretending the idea needed some serious consideration.

"Hey!" Henry gasps and then laughs.

"Never," I confirm. "But seriously, how often are you getting these headaches?"

"Babe, I promise, they're getting better. They've got me on an elimination diet, so we'll have this figured out in no time. I'm also going in after the holidays for a scan just to be safe." He steps forward, grabbing me by the arms, forcing me to look into his eyes. "I promise, I'm taking care of it, and there's nothing to worry about."

But I am worried. I love Henry, and I can't stand the idea of him being sick. "Maybe I should fly home with you."

"No!" he exclaims. "Don't get me wrong, I'd love to have you home with me, as my personal nurse, but you need this. And honestly, it's either work or rest for me these days. You'd be bored out of your mind."

"You need to let me know if things get worse, and I'll come home. Promise me," I demand.

Henry laughs, pulling me close and hugging me tight, "I promise, if I get worse, you can come home. But I won't get worse. I'm already feeling much better. I think the elimination diet's working."

We turn and walk out the room, Henry pulling the door closed behind us. "So tell me, how ready are you for the show?" He changes the subject as I link my arm through his, preparing to cross the street.

"I actually have all of the designs sketched, a few designs are completed and some of the other pieces are taking form. My biggest problem now is that I don't have any room to work," I explain.

"What do you mean?"

"I have fabrics bursting from all corners of my room. What I really need is a studio with a bunch of figures. I'm constantly having to reuse the same figure, and I spend most of my time looking for the right thread because it's buried under my masses of supplies."

I look up at Henry; it's obvious his wheels are spinning.

"What are you thinking?" I ask, knowing him all to well.

"Just brainstorming solutions," he replies. That's Henry —always trying to fix whatever problem I have.

"It's not a big deal, babe. It will be a great story to share when I'm a famous designer one day."

"Ahhh!" Emmie shrieks as she emerges from the entrance of the gallery, Olivia on her hip. "Henry, we're so glad you're here."

Colin follows close behind her, reaching out to take the baby from her, allowing Em to close in for the hug. She wraps her arms around Henry. I can tell he's not sure how to respond. Henry is more like me when it comes to affection from people. We're fine with one another, but an 'outsider' makes us terribly uncomfortable. Emmie is family to me now; it is time he learned to accept her as the same.

"Hello, wow," he says, smiling as Emmie pulls away, staring at him. "What a warm welcome."

"Are you two hungry? I'll warn you, the entire place smells of pork. I threw some meat in the crockpot when you left earlier so we could have carnitas tonight," Emmie explains. In true Emmie fashion, she continues talking. I notice whenever she has guests she rambles on incessantly.

"I'm not sure if Henry has ever eaten food from a crockpot," I interject.

The group falls silent, and everyone turns to look at me in disbelief. Henry's brow furrows.

"What?" I ask. "Your family isn't exactly the crockpot type."

"I'm not from outer space, sweetheart," he laughs. "I got through college thanks to a slow cooker." I wonder how I don't know this detail.

We head inside, the flow of conversation never stopping. They ask him about his work, about New York, all the things that are part of the world I used to be a part of. I suddenly start feeling insecure, like I don't have a home. *Am I a New Yorker? Do I belong in Texas now? Good Lord, Paige, who in the hell are you?*

We move our way through the gallery, back into the kitchen area, and the small dining nook off to the side. I suddenly realize Christian is nowhere to be found. Even though I'm nervous about them officially meeting, I'm also looking forward to getting it over with and moving on with our vacation together.

"You've got an amazing set up here." Henry remarks.

"It works for us right now, but if our family gets any bigger, we might have to think about a house." Colin explains. "For now, though, it works really well for us."

"So, Paige tells me your brother has a shop right next door." Henry says. I'm surprised by his topic transition.

Colin looks at me, then back at Henry. I can tell the subject shift makes Colin uncomfortable. "Yeah, I'd planned to turn the space next to this into additional living quarters, but when Christian came back, he decided he wanted to give his carving business a try. It seemed to work out for everyone."

"You're a very generous brother to simply give him the space like that," Henry comments, leaning over and looking out the window, his words feel a little sharp.

"Well, he does pay rent for the space, so I'm not really

sure if that's very generous." I can sense a tone of defensiveness in Colin's voice. "So sorry you won't be able to meet him on your visit, though."

"What?" I gasp before thinking. The entire group looks at me. "I mean—I don't understand. He didn't tell me he'd be gone."

"Oh, it was last minute. He got a call this afternoon that the rush order he was working on needed to be delivered right away. Apparently he couldn't find a delivery company that could take it on such short notice, so he decided to deliver it himself," Colin explains.

The group is quiet as I contemplate the information. That makes no sense. In the entire time I've been here, Christian has not left to make a single delivery. I know I heard him in the courtyard when we got back. Is he trying to be rude to Henry on purpose? Is he playing games of some kind? I'm not impressed and actually quite pissed off about his behavior. I thought we were past this kind of crap.

"Ah well, more carnitas for us," Henry says with a smile.

I shake my head. Why am I letting Christian get to me? If he wants to act like a complete ass, then that is his choice. The man I am going to marry is here, spending time with my closest friends. I'm not about to let my ex ruin it.

"So, Colin, I noticed the space across the street is for rent," Henry comments.

Colin looks at him, puzzled. "The old Stone Mill Bakery?" he asks.

Pressing his lips together, Henry shakes his head. "I

don't know. Would that be the one a few doors down from the inn?"

"Yeah, that's it," Emmie replies.

"Do you know the story on it?" Henry asks, and I find myself just as clueless as the rest of the group.

"The Meyer family owns the space. The parents ran the bakery for forty years—until they were too old. The kids didn't want to go into the family business so they closed up shop. They've been trying to rent it out for the past six months. Why?" Colin questions.

"Do you think they would consider renting it out for a month?" Henry asks.

Colin tilts his head. "Just a month?"

"Paige needs some place to spread out, and if it's just sitting there, I thought they may consider letting her use the space. I'm happy to pay a month's rent, of course."

"Henry—" I say. "Are you serious?"

"Of course, I want this show to be perfect for you, and if you need more room to work, then let's find you some space."

"Well, yeah, I'm sure they'd be happy to rent it out for a month," Colin says, smiling. "I'll call them first thing tomorrow."

"Thanks, I'd appreciate that."

I bury my head in Henry's chest, fighting back tears. He's always thinking about me. I wish I could give him a piece of what he's given me, but I don't even know where to begin. He has this instinct when it comes to taking care of me. I'm not a woman who allows herself to be cared for. My mother never took care of me, I took care of Christian, and for my entire life, I was used to this role.

I take a deep breath, concentrating on purging thoughts of Christian from my mind. Henry is my soul mate, and this visit is exactly what I need to remember that.

∼

CHAPTER 13

I'M NOT SURE how long I've been laying here, in this bed, staring at the curtains blowing in the open window, lost in my thoughts. I took Henry back to the airport earlier this morning. I told him I wanted to go home with him. I'd been away long enough, and I was home sick.

He wouldn't hear of it. He told me there were far too many distractions in New York, and if I am honest with myself, I know he's right. I have a circle of friends there that always have a hard time of taking no for an answer. If I went home, I would find myself at a club every night, never working on my designs. But I don't care, being away from Henry for a month was tolerable, but I feel like I've reached my limit.

While he was here, he managed to rent the space across the street, and we moved most of my stuff in, except, of course, what's in Christian's shop since he never came back. My thoughts drift to him, in an instant outrage consumes me again.

Christian has always had a way of figuring out the perfect ways to hurt me. He makes me think we're friends. That our past is behind us, that I don't have to worry about all the baggage of our previous relationship. He even told me he was excited to meet Henry, and then he disappears. I don't know why I thought he'd actually changed.

Suddenly I hear a door slam. Hopping to my feet, I make my way to the window. I lean out, searching for the source. My stomach twists as I see Christian walking around the corner, and with a jingle of his keys, opening the door to his studio.

The anxiety in the pit of my stomach quickly shifts into sour, hot anger. Christian behaves the way he does because nobody ever calls him out on it. I mean, really, should everyone walk on eggshells because he manages not to binge drink these days? Being a recovering alcoholic doesn't give you a license to be a complete asshole.

I race to the bedroom door, no longer moping about Henry heading home. I'm on a mission now … a mission to set Christian Bennett straight. If nobody else is going to tell him how immature his behavior can be, then I'll be happy to step in and take care of what needs done. He's the one who reached out to me, who wanted to be friends. Well, he's about to get a dose of what a real friend does— they tell you the things that are sometimes hard to hear.

Thudding down the stairs, I don't say anything to Emmie as I brush past her, the heat now emanating from my face. She might have said something as I walk out the back door, but I can't be sure as the blood pulsing in my ears is deafening.

I don't knock, and I don't hesitate. I throw open the door to Christian's studio and walk in as if I own the place. He is on the other side of the room, and when he catches sight of me he freezes.

"Christian Bennett," I say sternly, cringing slightly as I quickly realize I sound like a raging bitch. I pause, considering my next words carefully. Then I remember why I'm so angry. He says nothing, only continues to stare at me.

"What's wrong with you? I mean it. I really want to know—what exactly is broken inside that thick head of yours?"

He shifts his weight from foot to foot, uncomfortable by my tone.

"Well? Are you just going to stand there, or are you going to say something?"

"I would say something if I had any clue what you were talking about," he answers calmly.

"Oh, please, don't play dumb with me. You knew exactly what you were doing from the moment I came here."

"No, really. I don't know why you're so angry," he insists.

I'm insulted that he thinks I'm so stupid. If this is how he wants to play it, though, I am more than happy to lay it all out for him. "I come down here with the intention of working and spending time with my best friend. I didn't even know you were here when I decided to come."

"And you're mad at me for what exactly?"

"Are you kidding me? You spend the last month telling me how we can be friends, and there's no reason for things to be weird between us. Then you take me to that damn bar and—Jesus, I don't even know what the hell that was."

"You were just as much a part of that as me."

"Let me finish!" I demand. "You even tell me that you want to be friends with Henry, and no sooner than he gets here, do you take off."

"Oh, that's what this is about," he huffs, taking a step closer to me.

"Yeah, now you suddenly get it. I mean, really, I thought we were past all this childishness," I grumble, crossing my arms and glaring at him.

"Childishness?" His mouth falls open. "I had a last minute delivery to make. I didn't know I was supposed to clear my schedule with you. I don't think that means I'm childish."

"You really must think I'm stupid. You leave the minute Henry gets here, and then suddenly get back as soon as he's gone. A delivery took four days?" I question, not hiding my disbelief.

"Actually, yeah. It was a day's drive there and a day back, and then they paid me to do the installation job. Some of the work had to actually be done on site. I shouldn't have to explain my business to you Paige," he snarls, turning and walking across the studio, retrieving some tools from a table.

"Oh my God, you're totally going to stick to your story, aren't you?" I snap, walking to the door. Before exiting, I look back at Christian, who is now staring at me, again. "What I don't get is, why the games? I told Henry you wanted to meet him. Was it just to make me look stupid? You really haven't changed, have you?"

I don't wait for him to answer. It doesn't matter what he says. I know he'll tell me whatever he thinks I want to hear—that's how Christian works, and I've had enough of it. I should have trusted my gut and left him in the past, where he belongs.

~

CHAPTER 14

"*P*AIGE? YOU IN here?" I hear Colin's voice call from the entry of the shop.

"Behind the counter," I yell back from the table where I set up the sewing machine.

"I've got some boxes for you," he explains. "Where do you want them?"

"Anywhere is fine," I answer. "Are they deliveries from Henry?" I've been expecting some of the sample books from Henry's grandmother. I need to confirm the color choices on the flowers, as well as make sure the linens are to my liking. I'm not really sure how a tablecloth can't be to one's satisfaction, but she is adamant I sign off on them.

"No, they're the boxes of fabric from Christian's." His name is like a punch to the gut. I pull my foot off the pedal of the sewing machine and stand up. I look at Colin who is now setting the boxes next to the various others along the wall.

"He's sending you to do his dirty work, huh?" I've

managed to avoid Christian for the past two days, which, considering he eats every meal with Colin and Emmie, has not been an easy task.

"Why are you so angry at him?" Colin finally asks. He usually stays out of our business unless he feels absolutely certain one of us is being a complete idiot. Based on his questioning, I can only assume he thinks that person is me.

"He needs to be held accountable for his behavior, Colin; nobody around here seems to do that," I say pointedly.

"Look, I don't know what you think he did wrong, but he really did have a delivery he had to go take care of."

"You can leave the boxes," I say, making it clear I have no desire to have this conversation with him. He leaves without another word.

Walking to the front window of the shop, I peer out across the street. My pride won't let me tell Colin I've already doubted my reaction with Christian. Two days to think about my blow up has made me realize there is probably a good chance I didn't respond in the best way. Christian and I always had a heated relationship. Both of us have tempers, which is probably why the passion between us was always so intense.

Christian had made a point I'm struggling with. Just because we're friends doesn't mean he has to run his schedule by me. In the courtyard I catch site of him playing with Olivia, spinning her around like she is on an airplane ride, her head tilted back in laughter. Colin walks over to join them.

Watching the boys like this, playing with Olivia, I start to actually feel guilty. Damn it! Maybe I am wrong.

As I exit the shop and make my way across the street, Colin turns to say something to Christian as he sees me. He grabs Olivia and heads into the gallery. My paranoia is heightened by the exchange, and I wonder what was said about me. *Seriously, Paige? Who are you? Since when do you give a damn what anyone thinks?* I try like hell not to cave to the insecurities I'm not even aware I have.

Approaching Christian, I feel a lump forming in my throat. He begins waving his arms in front of his face before saying, "Whoa, truce, before you bite my head off again. I didn't think you'd want to see me, but you might need what was in those boxes. That's the only reason I sent Colin over, all right?"

I give a half smile, then with a deep swallow, proceed to deliver as sincere an apology as I can, still not fully convinced he hadn't avoided Henry and I on purpose.

"I may have overreacted the other day."

"Wait, was that an apology? It's so hard to tell with you."

"Funny," I groan with a glare.

"It's fine," Christian says flatly, turning and walking away from me, toward his wood shop. "I shouldn't have promised to meet Henry and then disappear without notice. That was rude, and I'm sorry," he adds over his shoulder.

Is he seriously walking away from me while we are having a conversation? I can't believe what I am seeing. He turns, gives me a short wave, and calls out for me to have a good night before heading inside. There is no way

WENDY OWENS

it just went down like that. I'm going to get to the bottom
of what is going on with him—sooner rather than later.
Walking up the narrow concrete path through the courtyard, I waste no time in pushing open the front door of
his studio. Christian is already walking into the back
room when I enter.

"Christian!" I yell after him.

"Did I forget one of the boxes?" he calls back, never
leaving the room he hides in.

With heavy steps, I cross the long room. "What is
going on with you?"

"Huh?" I hear him groan from the other side of the
wall.

I rush across to the opening of the back room. He's
looking at me, his eyebrows lifted, distressed by my presence. "Something is up with you. For a month we're fine,
hanging out even, and I thought we were actually
becoming friends again. Then you ditch us when Henry
comes."

"So we're back to this again?"

"No, I mean—I just apologized, and then you walked
away. What the hell is your deal?"

Christian looks at the large chunk of wood in front of
him. "I don't have a deal. What I have is a lot of work to
do, so if you don't mind, can you tell me how I should
have reacted so I can get back to it?"

Using every ounce of energy I have, I refuse to give
him the satisfaction of me losing my temper and shouting
at him. "I do mind. I mind that you act like my friend
when you're clearly interested in being anything but.
Jesus, are you drinking again?"

That comment clearly gets his attention. He lifts his chin, dropping the chisel in his hand to the floor and races across the room, his jaw clenched tight. "You should really be careful what you say. I haven't touched a drop since Olivia, and I told you that. You can do a lot of damage to someone with unfounded accusations."

"Then why are you acting so strange?" I push, remorseful for my words.

He looks away, frustrated.

I reach out and grab his arms.

"Tell me, what's going on? Did I do something?" I ask.

He hesitates, then says, "I thought I could handle this, handle you, but I can't."

"What are you talking about? What did I do?" I beg.

He looks down at the ground, tracing shapes with his shoe in the sawdust on the floor. Then, looking up at me, he says something that changes everything. Something that can never be undone. "I don't think us being friends is such a good idea."

"I don't understand what changed. Is this because I yelled at you? Is it about what happened at the bar?"

He shakes his head, struggling with something he doesn't want to say.

"Please, just tell me."

"I did have a rush order when Henry came, that part was true. But … I had time to stay and talk with him before I left."

"So why didn't you?"

"I saw you two in front of the inn," he says. I remember hearing him working in the courtyard, but I hadn't seen him. I wonder at what point he saw us.

"So?" I continue. "You knew he was coming."

"Knowing you're in love with another man is one thing, seeing you in his arms is another."

"No," I say, my head now shaking wildly. I raise a finger and point it at him. "You can't do this to me. You can't tell me you're okay with Henry, then get all weird on me."

"Jesus, Paige, you had to know," his voice cracks.

"Know what?"

"Why do you think I've been over at Colin and Em's every spare second since you got here?"

"You always are, that's what you do," I insist.

He shakes his head. "No, it's not. I'm there because I feel whole again when I'm around you."

"No, that's not right."

"I thought maybe, the other day, with the way you reacted when we danced, you might have felt it, too. But then, when I saw you with him, I realized I was wrong." His voice was quiet as he spoke.

"You can't do this to me," I plead. "I thought I was getting my friend back.

"You think I want to feel this way? When I saw him take you inside, and you didn't come back out, I—I couldn't think about it anymore. I loaded up my truck and got the hell out of here."

"What we had is over, Christian. I thought we both understood that."

Pressing his open palms against his face, he pulls downward, stretching out his expression as he does, clearly frustrated with the situation. "I was wrong. It was never over for me. We were never over."

And before I know it, we're having the post break up conversation we never had. "You were the one who told me to leave all those years ago," I remind him.

"Did you ever even turn around?" he asks with a rattle.

"What?" I can hardly believe we are saying the things we are, but as long as we are here, in this place, there are answers I want, too.

"I always wondered, that day you left, did you ever look back?" he asks again.

"You know I'm not the type to look back," I answered honestly.

"No, I suppose not," he says softly, before hanging his head.

"Oh my God, you are so not allowed to act all sad and rejected. You were the one who told me to leave," I snap, outraged by his reaction.

"I know. It's probably the biggest regret of my life." His words make all the hair on my entire body stand up straight. But I know better. Emmie told me all the things Christian was up to since our breakup. He didn't live like a man who regretted his choice.

"Please, don't act like you pined after me all these years. I know exactly what you were up to after we split. You forget my best friend is married to your brother."

"Oh, I never forgot. Half the stuff I told Colin to tell Em was just me hoping all the details would drive you crazy."

"Are you insane?" I ask, not believing a word he is telling me.

He shrugs his shoulders. "I was a little out of my mind at the time."

"You said you became a roadie because of a girl."

"Yeah, you were that girl. I went all over this country trying to forget you. It didn't work."

I cross my arms. If he wants to have this conversation, he is going to have to own up to some truths. "I know you were with other women; they weren't all stories."

"You're right. Neither of us has been alone since we split. But why do you think I was never in the same town for more than a week? Why do you think another women never stuck?" Christian asks me directly.

I turn my head and don't reply. I don't know how to reply. These are the things I had wondered since we broke up. "Damn it, Paige. If I stood still too long, all the memories of you, of us, I knew they'd catch up to me. I was afraid if I slowed down I'd have to think about what I'd lost."

"And what exactly is that?"

He moved in close—so close I could feel his heat near me. "My whole world."

Instinctively I push him away, but he grabs my wrists, pulling me in close again.

"Let go of me," I demand, trying to break free.

"Will you hear me out?" he asks, not releasing me. I struggle more, but the more I struggle, the tighter his grasp becomes. "Promise you'll listen to what I have to say."

"Fine!" I shout. "Now let me go."

He does as I request, and I stumble back a couple steps, widening the gap between us to a comfortable distance.

"I always wanted to tell you what was going on with me, but I could never find the words." I stand silently, listening, trying not to look him directly in the eyes, my heart now racing. "I know I had a problem. I drank to forget what I'd lost, and in the end, I lost more than I could ever have imagined."

"You'd stopped drinking for so long, and I never understood why you started again," I say.

"My brother is the strongest man I've ever known. I used to think my dad was the strong one, and when he died I'd missed out on life somehow." His eyes are now wet with the tears he's holding back.

"But Colin, he helped me so much. He was tough on me, but I always knew I could rely on him. When he got serious with Emmie it felt like losing my dad all over again. I was going to be alone."

"But you had me. You were never going to be alone," I say.

"I didn't realize that until it was too late," he replies softly.

"I tried to stay, to help you, but you kept pushing me away." I want to hold him, to convey all those things I'd felt years ago, but I refrain, not wanting to cross any more lines.

A silence lingers between us, before he takes a small step forward, looking into my eyes. "I'm not pushing you away now."

I feel I might throw up at any second. Christian is saying the things I would have given anything to hear a few years ago. But things have changed, and this can't be happening now. I've moved on. "Sometimes we break things, and they can't be fixed."

A silence hangs between us. I try to resist the question

on my mind, but it's plagued me for too long. "Why didn't you come after me? You had years."

"I knew you wouldn't take me back until I got my act together. By the time I figured out all the messed up things in my head, you were with him," Christian explains.

"You should have tried," I say, surprising myself.

"I'm trying now. It feels like you still love me, too."

I shake my head, blinking slowly. "I'll always love you, but—" I take a deep breath. "I'm *in love* with Henry, and I want to be his wife."

"Are you—"

"I should go," I interrupt. "If you think we can be friends, I'm here. But that's it."

I don't wait for Christian to respond. All I know is that I have to get out of this place immediately. My head is starting to spin. I leave as fast as I can, racing across to the space Henry had secured for me. I can't look at Emmie right now. She will know something is up, and I'm not ready to answer some of the questions she'll ask.

I need to work. Work will clear my head. It has to.

~

CHAPTER 15

I DON'T RECALL actually leaving Christian's shop. I don't even remember my walk back over to my temporary workspace. Hell, to be quite honest, the past few hours have been a blur. Holding up a leather vest, I examine the exterior seaming. It's impeccable. Perhaps I do my best work under duress.

Suddenly I realize my phone is ringing. It's a repeating segment of an Incubus song, "I Miss You." It's Henry. It doesn't cross my mind not to answer; instead, the thing I want most is to hear his voice. To reaffirm he's the man I want to spend the rest of my life with.

Answering my phone, I lift it to my ear, and in a daze, I say, "Hello?"

"Paige, hi babe," he says, sounding tired.

"I want to come home," I didn't even know the thought was going through my mind until I say it. But now that I have, it is the only thing that makes sense to me. At home there's no Christian, no confusion.

"What?" Henry asks, surprised.

"I mean it, I don't want to be away any longer. I want to come home."

"Honey, what's going on?"

"Nothing," I insist. "I miss you, I miss our home. Please, I just … I want to come home." Part of me wants to hold nothing back, to tell him everything, but I know I can't. I can't tell him that I've been having feelings for a man who I just found out is still in love with me.

The line is silent. Why isn't he saying anything? I just told him that I wanted to be there with him, and he's saying nothing.

"Hello?" Is he even still listening?

"I don't know what to say. I miss you, too. But—"

"But what?" I huff. "You wanted me to come down here so I could work on the wedding plans and my show. Well, I can tell you no wedding plans are getting done. I spend half my time helping Emmie with the baby or the gallery."

"So tell her you can't," he suggests.

"Why don't you want me to come home?" I ask, annoyed by his reaction and not wanting to share my true motivation.

"That's not it at all. I just think it's better for you if you stick it out a few more weeks," he continues.

"I can't. I need to come home," I insist.

He sighs heavily.

"What?" I huff.

"Nothing."

"No, that was a pretty big sigh for it to be nothing," I argue.

"We just rented out that studio space. Why wouldn't you have told me this while I was there?"

"Oh, so this is about some rent you paid for a place. I see."

"No, don't do that. You know I don't care about the money. It's … it doesn't make any sense. You were fine when I left, and now, it's suddenly an emergency for you to get back to New York." I'm not happy with his answer. In fact, the more we talk, the more I want to reach through the phone and strangle him.

"Jesus, just forget it," I snap. Leave it to Henry to dig deeper.

"Don't shut down on me." Ugh, I hate when he says that, because usually because he's right.

"What's going on with you?" I demand, turning the microscope away from me.

"Huh? What are you talking about?"

I want to hang up. This is not the conversation I planned on having when I answered the phone. I wish I hadn't even mentioned coming home at this point. Fighting with Henry makes me feel terrible, and it's honestly the last thing I need right now. "Never mind," I grumble.

"You can't just throw a grenade out there and walk away," he says. "What do you mean, what's going on with me? I don't understand. What have I done wrong?"

"It's nothing. Forget I said anything," I request, trying to dismiss the comment.

"No, damn it, Paige! You always do this. You can't put something out there and just let it linger. Explain what you mean."

"Don't yell at me."

"I'm not yelling," he insists, calming his tone.

"Well," I begin. "Maybe you're not yelling, but you're making me really uncomfortable."

"Then just tell me what you meant," he presses.

"Fine. God, I don't know why you always have to push me so much. But if you want to know, I'll tell you."

"Please, do."

"Every time we talk it seems like you're more and more distracted. It's like you could care less that I'm gone. I'm starting to think you prefer it that way."

"Are you serious? Am I the only one who was there last week? I thought we had an amazing time."

"Yes, we did, but—now, when I tell you I want to come home, it's pretty obvious you don't even want me there."

"Do you really think that?" he asks gently.

I sit silent, thinking about his question. I don't believe it. I know he loves me, and I know he'd rather I be at home with him. I also know he just wants what's best for me, and that's why he's pushing me to stay. But on some level, it infuriates me that his desire to not be away from me isn't overwhelming his desire for me to succeed. Selfishly, I want his world to stop when I'm not there. Granted, then I would probably think he was clingy. Damn it, I don't know what I want.

"Well?" Henry asks again.

"No," I admit. "I just can't do all of this without you. It's too much."

"Then how about we hand some of the wedding details off to Grandmother. I could care less what the wedding looks like, as long as you're there with me."

I feel warmth envelop me at his words. I don't know why I freak out and try to make a mess of things all the time. He will always love me, and I him. "Yeah, that might be good," I agree.

"How about you give it another week, and if you want to come home after that, then we'll get you on a plane right away."

"All right," I relent. I can do a week.

"Paige?" I hear Emmie's voice call out as she steps in through the front door. She's carrying a plate of food; this has become our routine in recent days.

"Over here," I yell from behind a pile of boxes. "Babe? I've gotta go. Dinner time."

"Okay, are we good?" Henry asks, uneasy that the conversation is coming to such an abrupt end.

"Yeah, I'm sorry I flipped out on you," I reply.

"Are you sure we're fine?"

"Yes, I promise."

"Okay, then go eat. I should probably do the same."

"I love you," I say softly.

"I love you, too, and goodnight."

As I hang up the phone, I look to see Emmie standing directly in front of me. From the expression on her face, I can see she already knows more than I wish she did.

"He told you?"

"Huh?" She tries to play ignorant, placing the plate of foil-covered food on the table next to us.

"Please, you're a terrible liar, so don't even try," I warn.

"I might have overheard Colin and Christian talking while I was cooking dinner."

"How much do you know?" I question.

135

"He told you he's still in love with you?" she inquires.

"Pretty much."

"What are you going to do?" I have no idea how to answer that question.

"What am I supposed to do with that? I told him I'm in love with Henry now. Then I got the hell out of there."

"What did Henry say?"

"I told him I want to come home, but he … he wants me to stay."

"Did you tell him what Christian said?"

"No!" I exclaim. "Do you think I'm crazy? That will only make him think something has been going on, when it hasn't. And besides, he's been weird enough lately."

"What do you mean?" she asks.

"I don't know. He seems distracted. Every time we talk he has to go because he's about to take a nap or something else. It just always seems like it's something," I explain.

"What do you think's going on?"

"I have no clue. Maybe it's work or his grandmother. I know she can be a nightmare, and I'm sure it's worse with the wedding getting so close and me out of town."

"So are you flying home?" she inquires, moving closer.

"Not yet. I promised Henry I'd at least give this another week."

"What about what Christian said?"

"What about it?" I ask, narrowing my brows in puzzlement.

"Have you thought about giving him another chance?" I can't believe she just asked me that question.

"When you were engaged to Colin did you ever

consider giving one of your exes another chance?" I ask, not masking my disgust.

"First of all, I've only been with one other man besides Colin, and he killed himself so that really wasn't an option," she reminds me. Damn it! She always has the my-ex-committed-suicide card, which makes most of my comparisons completely irrelevant.

"You get what I mean. I'm committed to Henry. I don't even know how you could ask me that." Emmie looks away quickly, and I can tell she's hiding something. "What?"

"Huh?" she mutters innocently.

"No, I know you! Spill it."

"I might have heard Christian tell Colin that he's not ready to give up on you."

"What the hell does that mean?" I ask, irritated.

"I think he's going to ask you out on a date."

"What? Well, that's too bad. I'm not going," I say firmly.

I pull the foil off the plate she brought me. Mashed potatoes, chicken breast, and green beans are placed neatly in even portions. The smell hits me, and I can't help but moan in delight. I skip the fork and dip a finger into the mashed potatoes.

"Umm …" Emmie begins, then stops herself.

I look at her, then demand, "What?"

Emmie shakes her head, and continues. "I don't think he's going to take no for an answer."

"He's just going to have to. Thanks for dinner, but I better get back to work." I'd had enough fun talking about Christian and his sociopathic behavior. Henry's right. I simply need to put my head down and get through the next few weeks. The only way Christian is going to distract me anymore is if I let him.

CHAPTER 16

*W*AKING UP AT six o'clock in order to avoid breakfast with the Bennett boys is starting to take a toll on my sanity. On one hand, I've been more productive in recent days than probably ever before, but on the other, I'm getting quite cranky. This morning when Henry called, I actually hung up on him.

This isn't normal behavior for us. All morning I hope he will call back, so that I can apologize. Why on Earth I feel like he is the one who needs to call me, I don't know. Perhaps it's just another instance of me not thinking rationally when I receive improper amounts of sleep.

Basically, I can trace all of the blame for the recent argument straight back to Christian. Had he not confessed his love to me, then I would not feel compelled to get up at an ungodly hour, missing precious hours of sleep, in order to avoid him. *Damn it Christian, is everything your fault?*

The door to my little studio space opens. I look up and —Jesus—it's him!

"What are you doing here?" I demand, disgusted that he would ruin my plans to completely avoid him for the remainder of my stay in Bastrop.

He walks in, with one hand behind his back, and pushes the door closed with his foot.

"I'm serious, you can't be in here. I'm working."

He reveals a bundle of fresh-cut flowers. The violets are a soft purple and touches of creams and whites are scattered about, acting as a perfect complement. "Truce?"

"Excuse me?"

"I come bearing gifts. I'd like a cease fire between us," he says, walking across the room. I want him to stop moving toward me. Every step he takes, I can feel the heat in the room increasing.

"Okay, whatever. We're fine. I just have a lot of work to do," I say dismissively, hoping he will catch the hint and turn to leave. He doesn't. In a few more seconds he is now only a few feet from me, looking around at all of the scraps of fabric on the table.

He pushes the flowers in my direction, but I wave my hands, unwilling to accept the gesture, for fear of what that might say to him.

"Please. I got them for you."

"I appreciate that, but I don't even have anything to put them in," I explain, still refusing them from his extended hands.

He drops his arms, staring at my face silently. I look around at my work, picking up a strip of fabric and trying to seem extremely busy again, in hopes he will leave. Instead, he places the bundle of flowers on the table between us and proceeds to walk around it. There is no longer a barrier between us, and my heart begins to race. I wish we weren't alone.

He lunges forward, and I hold my breath, close my eyes, and prepare for his touch. But there is nothing. I lift my lids and realize he is leaning over to pick up one of the garments I've been working on, and not to touch me.

"Are you all good?" he asks me with a confused stare.

"Yeah, I'm fine," I insist. "I just have a lot of work to do, so if you don't mind ..." I look to the door, trying to make the request clearer with my eyes.

"This is really gorgeous, Paige. These tones, they're almost like what you find in cedar planks," he comments, examining the garment closer.

My head tilts. "I was going for a wood tone in my selection of the fabric." Suddenly I'm not thinking about the fact that Christian, my ex who is still in love with me, is standing in front of me. I am instead excited that my design resonates in the way I intended.

"Here," I continue. "I was going to pair this leather vest with it." I turn and reach over around behind the sewing machine to retrieve the piece I'd been working on the previous evening. "I think the black will contrast it well. And I like the idea of black leather and old woods. I want to design a metal chevron necklace to go with it, but the jewelry will have to wait until I actually finish the garments."

"That's going to look incredible. Jesus, I knew you were talented, but my God," he comments, reaching out with a free hand to run his fingers across the stitching on the vest.

"Oh please, this is nothing. I can't exactly make furniture out of a hunk of wood." Did I just say that? I want to cut out my tongue. What in the hell am I doing? He needs to get out of here—the sooner the better.

He drapes the tunic dress across the chair next to us, never taking his eyes off me. The silence feels uncomfortable, and my eyes dart around the room, trying to avoid his stare. I can see he does not feel compelled to look away. His stare is intense, and though I fight as hard as I can to avoid it, eventually I'm caught. He steps closer, licking his lips and narrowing the gap between us to only a little more than a foot.

The intensity in his eyes is more than I can bear; I force myself to stare at his dimple, avoiding the penetrating glare. But that only makes me want to press my lips against the small cavern.

"We never got to finish our talk," he says in a soft, but deep and raspy voice.

My back is up against the table. There is nowhere for me to go, and nowhere for me to look accept at him.

"There's nothing to talk about," I say, trying to find an escape.

"I think there is. If you don't want to talk, then just listen," he continues.

"Christian," I whisper, wishing with everything in me he'll stop and walk away, because I know I don't have the strength to make him stop.

"When I saw you with him, it was the most intense pain I've ever felt. I managed to fool myself into believing I could get over you, but I can't. And I don't think you're over me."

"I'm getting married," I say firmly.

"That's not what I said. I said, I think you still love me, too."

His words hang between us. I back up, standing on my tiptoes, and place my bottom on the table to increase the distance between us, if only by inches. He uses the opportunity to move in closer, maneuvering in between my legs, and pressing his body against mine.

"Tell me I'm wrong," he says, his hot breath now on my cheek.

I freeze. I can't think, say, or do anything. Reaching up with one hand, he tucks a stray hair, which hangs in my face, behind my ear. I tell myself to push him away, but my arms aren't listening to me. Instead, I find myself licking my lips, wishing for a taste, just once more.

I part my lips, and I close my eyes and let go, giving all control to him. I can taste the bitterness from my morning coffee in my saliva. My chest begins to ache, and my stomach groans in anticipation of what might be coming next.

I notice my hands clenched into balls of sweaty fists. Opening them, I rub my palms against my jeans. I feel Christian grab my hands. I still don't open my eyes. He forcefully places them on his hips, pressing hard against me now. In an instant I'm turned on, and the desire starts to overwhelm me.

What am I doing? The question pushes its way into my thoughts, but is quickly shoved out when I feel his lips graze my cheek.

He whispers, "You want this. I can tell."

Damn it! Is he right? My body seems to think so.

"I won't kiss you unless you want me to," he moans.

143

WENDY OWENS

I turn my head into his lips without hesitation. I don't want him to talk; I want so much more. At last the warmth of his mouth is against mine. The initial sensation is different than it had been while we were together. Christian hadn't had facial hair during our entire relationship, and now he maintains consistently thick stubble. At first I find it unsettling, but when his lips part and the wetness of his tongue rushes into my mouth, all I want is for the kiss to never end.

He wraps his arms around me, pulling me in, pressing his chest against me, gripping me with his strong arms. I can feel his muscles flexing as we kiss. He's enjoying it as much as me. I wrap my legs around his hips and run my hands up his back, digging my fingers through his shirt, into his flesh. When I do, I feel him moan with delight into my mouth.

The sensation nearly sends me into wild spasms. I throw my head back and, using every muscle in my body, push him away, hopping to the ground, quickly making my way around to the other side of the table.

"Stop!" I gasp.

"If that's what you want," he says, delivering a devilish grin before adding, "but your body was telling me something else."

My voice quivers as I say, "I'm engaged."

"I thought we already established this."

"It doesn't seem to be registering for you."

"I guess we both know what this means." He smirks.

"We do?"

"You'll just have to tell him about us," he says in a sincere tone.

Now I'm angry. Us? Who said there was an *us*, and

144

what makes him think he can just come in here, turn on his sex mojo, and tell me what to do?

"No!" I shout.

"What? But—"

"You kissed me, and it was a mistake. Damn it! There is no us!"

"You can keep telling yourself that, but it won't make it any truer."

"I love Henry," I insist.

"Then why did you kiss me?" he asks me pointedly.

I hesitate. I don't know the answer. I did kiss him, and I loved it. I also want more. I want to rip his clothes off right here and have my way with his incredible body. But I can't. I can't because the idea of hurting Henry in that way makes me sick to my stomach. That has to mean something about what I feel for him.

"I don't know—maybe I do still have *some* feelings for you. But it doesn't change the fact that I love Henry," I finally concede.

He stares at me with a hungry look, and I worry he might swoop in for another kiss. "I think it changes everything. Is it fair to marry Henry when you'll be thinking about me for the rest of your lives together?"

"Wow." It's suddenly becoming much easier to push Christian away. "Aren't you full of yourself?"

"No, I'm serious," he argues. "Just hear me out. Maybe it is just a lingering attraction, and nothing could ever truly rekindle between us. But don't you owe it to yourself and to Henry to figure that out?"

I laugh. "So you're trying to tell me I owe it to Henry to sleep with you?"

"Whoa there, tiger," Christian says, waving his arms. "I don't think anything was said about sleeping with anyone. I mean, hey, I'm game if you are, but I was thinking of taking it a bit slower—maybe spend some time together under a different pretense, see if there's anything to this."

"We spent most of last month together," I remind him.

"I know, and that was fun, but it was as friends. It was also before I realized you still had feelings for me—"

"An attraction, not feelings," I argue.

"If you say so," he chimes, presumptuously.

"So what are you saying?"

"Go out on three dates with me," Christian proposes. "If at the end of those three dates you aren't madly in love with me again, then I will give you and Henry my blessing."

"I'm not doing that."

"Why? Scared of what you might discover?"

"No!" I shout, my face growing hot.

"Then why not?"

I hesitate; his suggestion has my head spinning. "I can't … I …" I huff, now completely flustered. "That's cheating, and I won't do that to Henry."

Christian stares at me. "I know how I feel about you, and I'm pretty confident that if you open yourself up to us, you'll find out you feel the same, but I don't want you to do anything you could possibly hate yourself for later."

"Then it's settled. You'll leave me alone for the rest of the time I'm here."

"Not so fast. What about we agree to three dates, but with ground rules. No sex, no kissing, just a G-rated date," he suggests as a solution.

I shake my head. This feels wrong, and my mind is telling me to tell Christian to get the hell out of my sight, so I can get on a plane and head straight home. "I don't know. What makes them a date?"

He takes a step back, widening the gap even more between us. "I promise, nothing physical. All I'm asking is you give me a real chance to win you back. If you go and marry him, without really knowing if we are truly over, it's like you'll never be able to completely give yourself to him. Do you really want to do that to Henry?"

I know what he's doing. He has always been a master at spinning things in the way he wants people to see them. And even though I know what he's doing, I can't believe what I find myself saying. "All right."

"Seriously?" he asks, surprised.

"Yes, but if you step out of line in any way, this little experiment is over. Got it?"

"Of course."

"And, after the three dates, when I'm still in love with Henry, you'll let this drop once and for all?"

"I give you my word. But by then, you'll be mine again," he says confidently, darting around the counter and out the door, yelling over his shoulder, "First date is this Friday at seven o'clock. I'll pick you up here."

As the door falls closed I'm suddenly light headed. I lean my body weight against the table to steady myself. *What just happened?*

CHAPTER 17

OLIVIA STUMBLES ACROSS the floor and begins pulling fabric samples out of one of the boxes lining the wall. I look over at Emmie, perched on a stool next to the table. This does not seem to bother her. I consider going over to stop the mini tornado, but decide she's having far too much fun to interrupt her.

"So you know this can only end in disaster?" Emmie says, before popping another grape into her mouth.

"Yes, you've told me every day for the past three days, so I'm starting to understand your opinion quite well," I say sarcastically, leaning over the table and snatching a grape from her hands.

"And since when do you have so much cleavage?" she asks me, staring at my chest.

I quickly stand, self consciously looking down at my body. "Hey, I have nice tits."

"That's not what I said," she corrects me. "You have amazingly perky, beautiful little tits, but that's not what's hanging out of that shirt. That is some major cleavage, girl."

I look down again, smile and reply, "I guess it's the bra."

"I thought this was supposed to be a pretend date."

"It is," I confirm, furrowing my brow.

"So you just want to blue-ball him."

I shrug. "I don't know, maybe." We both laugh before I add, "If he crosses the line, then this stupid little experiment is over. That's the deal. And if my cleavage is too much for him to resist, then I guess our first date will be our last."

"Yup, disaster," Emmie says again, looking at Olivia who has now made her way over to the next box of samples. It is probably the quietest and most content I've ever seen the child.

"It's really not a big deal, Em. I'll go, prove I don't love him anymore, and that will be the end of it."

"So you told Henry about it then?"

"No!" I exclaim. "He wouldn't understand."

"What on Earth would he not understand about his fiancée going on a date with another man?" she teases.

"Oh, you know—"

"Good evening, ladies," Christian says as he walks in through the door. "Don't you all look beautiful."

"Oh please, sucking up doesn't work with me anymore," Em huffs, waving a hand in her brother-in-law's direction.

"Me? I'd never," he insists smugly.

"I'm wearing yoga pants that are a size too small for

me, and I have half of Olivia's dinner on my shirt. Shut it down, Romeo."

I can't help but laugh.

"Come on Olivia," Emmie continues, walking over and scooping her daughter into her arms. "Let's let these two insanely dysfunctional people get on with their disastrous evening."

"Gee, thanks sis," Christian says as she walks past him.

"Anytime," Em replies. God, I love that girl. She might be the only other snarky bitch who can hold her own with the Bennett brothers.

Christian waits for the door to close before turning and looking in my direction. I make my way around the counter and stand for a moment, waiting to see if he realizes I'm wearing the piece he'd noticed from the collection.

"Wow," he gasps, drinking me in.

"You don't look so bad yourself," I say, impressed by the gray blazer and button-up shirt. Though it is paired with jeans and boots, I can only assume it is fitting for what he has chosen to do for our evening.

"Shall we?" he asks, extending an arm to take my hand.

"Of course," I reply, grabbing my leather satchel and throwing it over my shoulder. Considering 'wow' is the only comment I get, I'm not sure he notices I'm wearing—.

My thought is suddenly cut short. "I'm honored you'd wear a piece from your new collection on our date." Strike that, he did notice.

"Yeah, I'll definitely be avoiding red wine this evening," I comment before giggling and making my way out the front door. "So, what are we doing?" I inquire eagerly. I hate to admit it, but part of me has been looking forward to this evening all week. Not that I think anything will actually come out of it, but it sure is going to be fun to see Christian try.

"I think you'll be pleasantly surprised," he replies with a smile.

I look up at him; I can see he's very pleased with himself. "Oh, that's how it's going to be."

"What?"

"You want to keep it a surprise."

"Surprises can be fun." He grins as I come to stand at the door of his truck across the street. I turn around and realize he isn't near me. Instead, he's on the sidewalk, watching me, just standing there with that crooked smile, his hands in his pockets.

"What are you doing?" I ask, puzzled.

"I'm heading to our date, what are you doing?"

"Huh?"

"We can walk," he explains.

"Oh, I see. So it's the steakhouse for dinner then," I say, thrilled I'd so easily uncovered his secret.

"Nope, not the steakhouse."

"What? That's the only place open this late on a Friday night on the strip … unless …" I start.

"Unless what?"

"You're taking me to the diner for dinner? That's a little low rent for a blazer, isn't it?"

"Did I say we are going to the diner?"

Oh my God! There are only two restaurants open on the strip past seven on a Friday. Unless we're walking a mile outside of town, which means I did not wear the right shoes, there are no other options.

"Fine, I give, where are we going?"

"You'll see," he says as he continues to casually stroll down the sidewalk. I can tell he knows it's pushing me to the brink not to know, and he loves every second. "Beautiful night, isn't it?"

I look up at the night sky. I'll be heading home to New York in a couple more weeks, preparing to begin my life as Mrs. Wallace and an image like this will no longer be part of my day. "Yes, it is." I sigh deeply.

"What is it?"

"I'm going to miss the stars. You just can't see them like this in the city, you know?"

"Yeah, but who knows, maybe you'll move down here," Christian suggests with a serious face. I immediately laugh, assuming he has to be kidding. He isn't.

"Christian!" I exclaim. "My life's in New York."

"And your life could just as easily be down here. Can you imagine watching Olivia grow up?"

"Yeah … I mean … it would be nice, but I'm a city girl. I wouldn't know how to handle living in Texas."

"You seem to be doing just fine to me," he adds, coming to a stop.

I turn and look up; we were at Baxter's. "They're closed," I remind him.

"Are they?" he asks mischievously, walking to the door and pulling it open.

"Oh—aren't you Mr. Important? You got them to stay open just for us, huh?"

"Not exactly," he says, leaving me guessing until the last moment.

I enter through the open door, looking around for other patrons. There are none. In fact, there are no waiters either—no staff of any kind. I follow Christian like a stray puppy, completely unsure what to expect.

"Hey man." I hear a voice from the far side of the room.

"Tito!" Christian exclaims. "This is Paige."

Christian steps to one side as I extend a hand in greeting. The man has black hair that's just beginning to gray at his temples, but he seems to still be quite young.

"I see what you mean. She's gorgeous," the man says, smiling at me as he shakes my hand.

"Why thank you," I reply with a tight-lipped grin and a glance at Christian.

"Well, I'll let you two get to it. Just lock up when you're done," Tito says, handing a cluster of keys to Christian. He turns and exits the building without another word. I'm even more perplexed than before.

"All right, what's going on?" I question, the suspense insufferable.

"Since I can tell it's killing you, I'll tell you. I'm going to make you dinner," he answers, turning and walking into the kitchen.

"What?" I gasp. "You can't cook."

"Actually," he begins, pulling out a large cast iron skillet from under the counter and placing it on top. "I know how to cook quite well."

"What in the hell is with Texas? Emmie can cook now, and you, too?" I laugh in disbelief.

"I learned before I came to Texas. If you want to stick

around as a roadie, you better make yourself useful, and that means learning how to cook. I had a great teacher, though. Mac."

"Did you just say Mac? What kind of name is Mac?" I ask, amused.

Christian looks at me disapprovingly; he is obviously sensitive about whoever this Mac character is.

"Sorry, was he like the old wise and elderly roadie who taught you the ropes?"

"No," he replies, pulling out a tray that is overflowing with veggies. "Mac is short for Mackenzie."

"Oh." I gulp. That isn't the response I'd expected. "Was she your girlfriend?" I ask, not sure I want to head down this path.

I see him smile; I want to kick myself for giving him the satisfaction. I tell myself I'm not jealous, no matter what he thinks.

"I think she wanted to be."

I think about his reply, slightly disgusted by it. "Too ugly for you? I can only imagine what a roadie chick looks like," I joke, trying to help him understand how shallow he sounds.

He shakes his head, not looking at me, as he continues to prepare the ingredients for what he's about to make. "No, she was actually quite beautiful."

I think about this for a moment. Perhaps I misunderstand the implication, "Oh—I see—so she was just a booty call, then?"

"Jesus, you don't think very much of me, do you?"

"Well, you did admit to being with a lot of women."

"First of all, I don't think I ever used the term, 'a lot.'

And second, Mac was a friend. I didn't want to do that to her," Christian explains.

"Do what?" I ask, confused.

"Really? You're going to make me say it?"

I squint my eyes, still unaware of what he's saying.

"Fine," he continues. "I was still hung up on you. I knew Mac and I would never work out, and since we were friends, I didn't want to put her through that. As long as I was still in love with you, I could never feel the same way she did."

"Wow, that's awfully noble of you," I say sarcastically, trying to diffuse the intensity of his statement.

"It worked out," he continues, ignoring my quip. "She ended up with some singer. I think his name is Jett."

"Mac and Jett, you can't be serious?"

"Yeah, apparently his mom was some huge Joan Jett fan. Actually their story is pretty amazing, but I'll save that for some other time," he teases.

I look at him; it is clear there's a lot about him that has changed. A lot I didn't know. There is an entire other life we've lived since we've been apart. I know I'm in love with Henry, and Christian will never be able to change that, no matter how many pseudo dates we go on. But even knowing that, part of me is glad I've agreed to this little arrangement. Once Christian realizes there isn't any hope for us, maybe there's a chance we can be friends again; and for that reason, I'm looking forward to getting to know him better.

"I have a feeling you have a lot of stories like the one with Mac and Jett," I comment, watching him as he scoops up the chopped veggies and places them in the cast iron skillet.

"Oh, please—I wasn't the one jetting around Europe for the past four years. How many Dukes or Princes did you get to propose?"

"There were a few."

"I'm sure." He smiles at me. I do love his smile. That was something that would always cheer up my day when we used to live in New York—so long ago now.

"Please, you know I'm kidding, right? I didn't have time to get serious with anyone."

"Except Henry."

"Yeah, I told you, we met on the flight back to the States," I remind him. Suddenly there's a tension in the room. Henry is probably the last thing we should be talking about. It only makes me think about how angry he will be that I agreed to such an idiotic proposal in the first place.

"So what are you making me?" I inquire, completely clueless.

"Don't you want it to be a surprise?"

"Oh God, no! No more surprises. Please, tell me."

"If you insist."

"I do, I'm starving," I say, clutching my stomach, as if it were wildly growling.

"No worries. Once these are all in the oven, I prepped some salads for us," he informs me proudly.

"Oh my, you are certainly well-prepared."

"What can I say? I'm a man who knows what he wants and will do whatever it takes to get it done."

"All righty—that sounded creepy," I joke.

"Agreed, sorry. I know you're not a huge meat fan, so I prepared a vegetarian-based feast. This is a twist on shepherd's pie."

"With mushrooms?" I ask inquisitively.

"Yup, with an Italian flare. It has a marinara base, which, by the way, I also made myself ahead of time. There is also some roasted eggplant, sautéed mushrooms, and then a cheesy polenta on top." As he explains the dish, I feel my mouth begin to water.

"Mmm …" I moan. "That sounds amazing."

"I'm not done, my lady. In the warming oven, as we speak, are cheese stuffed poblano chiles that have been roasted and battered, then deep fried for a little crispiness. When you have an entire kitchen like this at your disposal, you can get very creative."

"You're going to have to tell me sometime what dirt you have on Tito to get the keys to this place for the night," I say with a huge grin.

His expression shifts into a serious one. "Never."

I laugh. "And what's for dessert?" As soon as the words slip out of my mouth I realize they came out in a way that can easily be construed as dirty. My eyes dart to his, and I smile. I can see it on his face—he heard the accidental inflection, but he wasn't about to take the bait.

Christian licks his lips before continuing, "How about we leave dessert a surprise?"

I nod. "I can handle one surprise, I suppose."

"Oh— you suppose?"

"Yes," I confirm with as much attitude as possible. Even if I know there is no hope for Christian's plan to win my heart back, it is nice being able to spend a few nights together, just enjoying each other's company the way we once did. God, we used to laugh so much. There were times I'd wake up with my sides sore because of how hard I'd laughed the night before.

He is a perfect gentleman all through dinner. He is true to his word, and there is no inappropriate physical contact between us during our, as he insisted on calling it, 'date.' As long as this is how things remain, I see no need to bother with telling Henry about Christian's antics. We'll go on the next two dates, and this silliness will be behind us.

I push myself away from the table, patting my stomach. "Wow, I'm stuffed." I then release a small belch, leaning my head to one side.

"Just as classy as ever, I see," Christian taunts.

"Hey, when you got it, you got it. What can I say?"

"So true," he says, glancing over his shoulder. "Ready for that surprise dessert?"

I groan, "Oh my God, I can't fit another bite."

"Not even if it's your favorite?"

I pause, investigating his expression. He can't possibly remember all these years later, can he? "No way," I say dismissively.

He walks into the kitchen and returns with a covered dish. I watch in disbelief as he reveals the most divine looking German chocolate cake.

"Shut up!" I exclaim.

"From scratch, just for my Paige," he boasts, placing the enormous cake in front of me. "Oh, I forgot a knife, I'll be right back."

"Don't bother," I call after him, picking up my fork and

proceeding to cut off the most massive hunk the utensil can hold before shoveling it into my mouth.

Christian busts out laughing at my display. With crumbs spraying out wildly, I defend myself, "It's German chocolate cake, which means it's not my fault." Of course he can't understand a word I say. He walks back over to the table, and I scoop off another bite, feeding him a taste. I don't even think about it. I should have, but I didn't.

He takes hold of my hand, guiding it in, as it nears his mouth. There's an electricity between us as our skin touches. *Damn it, Paige, no physical contact, and this one is your fault.*

I drop the fork and back away. I know he can see the horror in my eyes. The regret. Even our hands touching is more than I am okay with.

"I better go," I say. "It's getting late.

"Paige, it was just some cake," he pleads.

"No— it was fun. It was a fun night. Thank you. I'm just tired, and I have a full day tomorrow."

"Please, I'll walk you back. I just need to lock up real quick."

"Don't be silly. You made dinner. I think I can walk a few doors down on my own." I don't wait for him to reply, but rather, I race out the front door as fast as I can, heading straight in the direction of the gallery and a safe, Christian-free place. The entire evening had been perfect. The food was delicious. He made me laugh, he shared stories, he listened, and then I had to go and screw it up at the end.

I tiptoe up the stairs, careful so Colin and Emmie don't hear me. It's not extremely late, but I know if Emmie finds out I am back, she'll want to ask me a million questions. I know this because I was the same way when she and Colin started dating.

I flop down on my bed, lying there for a moment, just staring up at the ceiling. My phone vibrates. Three missed calls from Henry. He'll have to wait until morning. I close my eyes for a second, and suddenly sleep envelops me.

CHAPTER 18

THE SUN POKES itself into my room. I reach out my arms, enjoying my morning stretch and yawn to the fullest, feeling my spine crack as I do. Immediately, I lean over and grab my phone, flipping through my music options. "Moth's Wings" by Passion Pit catches my eye, and I hit play.

As I hop to my feet, my hips and hair swaying to the music, an image of a bad eighties movie flashes through my mind, and I can't help but smile. In this moment I don't really care if I look absolutely ridiculous. I'm not a morning person, but on this particular morning, I've awoken feeling absolutely amazing, and I'm not about to squander it.

There is a knock at the door, but I don't notice, surrounded by the music and the moment. "Work it, girl!" I hear Emmie's voice behind me.

Panting, I turn and see her smiling back at me, leaning against the frame of the door, watching my every move. I bend in half at the waist, laughing, and attempt to hide my face.

"Oh no—please don't stop on my account," she insists.

"Shut up," I growl, collapsing onto the bed, snickering.

"I came up because I thought something must be wrong," Emmie continues, standing upright and moving directly across from me.

"Huh? What are you talking about?"

"You know it's Saturday, right?"

"And?"

"You don't wake before noon on Saturday, let alone start your mornings off dancing," Emmie teases.

"Maybe I'm becoming a morning person."

"Yeah," she scoffs. "Somehow I doubt that. Does this mean your date with Christian went well last night?"

"It wasn't a date," I correct her, avoiding the question.

"When everyone is calling it a date except for you, it doesn't make it any less of a date."

"Whatever," I add dismissively, grabbing my phone and flipping through the music choices. "Bruises" by Chairlift is my next selection. I press the genius playlist option, and then return the phone to the speaker dock on the nightstand.

"Well?" Emmie pushes. She clearly isn't going to let this rest until she gets all the details.

"Since when does Christian cook?" I inquire, thinking back on the evening.

"He's good, isn't he?"

"Not bad."

"How was the German chocolate cake?" she asks.

I look at her, narrowing my glare. "How did you know?"

"Really? I knew what he was planning days before you did."

"And you didn't tell me?"

"And suffer the wrath of Colin and Christian? No way, you're on your own with this one, girl," Emmie replies, collapsing on the bed next to me.

I prop myself up and look into her eyes, watching for any sign she might be hiding something else from me. "What does he have planned for date number two?"

She grins. "I thought they weren't dates."

"You know what I mean," I huff, falling back.

"Actually—I have no idea what he has planned for your next date."

I groan, frustrated with the entire situation. Even if he somehow manages to get me to concede, I might still have some sort of feelings for him, it doesn't change how I feel about Henry. Christian and I lost our shot at a happily ever after.

"You really have no intention of telling me how it went last night, do you?"

"It went fine," I offer.

"I'll take that as you had wild and crazy sex and that you ate cake off each other's naked bodies."

"If you had balls, I'd kick you in them."

Emmie laughs. "Then tell me, or I'll have to let my imagination loose on the evening."

"Jesus, you're relentless."

She grins confidently, grabbing a pillow, and wrapping

her arms tightly around it. "Yup, but that's one of the many reasons you love me."

I prop my back up against the small headboard, the metal frame digging into my shoulder blade. Shifting, moving another pillow into place behind me, I debrief my friend of the evening's details. I tell her about the conversations that were had, the delicious meal he prepared for me, and then the way I ruined everything.

She stares at me, contemplating the details. I wish she'd say something, anything. "Well?" I prod.

"So he didn't kiss you or violate your rule in any way?" she clarifies.

"No, he was a perfect gentleman."

"And you freaked out because his hand touched yours?" she continues, a disbelief in her voice.

"Yeah, that's what I said. Why?"

"I'm just trying to figure out who in the hell you are?"

"What the hell?"

She shakes her head, and then locking eyes with me, explains, "You're the girl who always does whatever she wants, no matter the consequences. You freaking graze his hand and you flip out? You're afraid, aren't you?"

"I am not afraid!"

"No, it … it makes sense now," she stammers, connecting the thoughts in her head. "You know you still love him, and that's why you're afraid. Jesus, how didn't I see it before?"

"You need to stop, I'm serious. You don't know what you're talking about," I warn.

She reaches out and scoops my hands into hers, squeezing tightly. "You helped me when I was afraid."

I pull away, standing and turning away from her. "I'm not kidding. You need to stop it!"

"Don't be pissed, I'm just telling you what I see," Emmie says defensively, shifting uneasily on the bed.

"These dates were a mistake," I say, beginning to pace.

"Probably," she agrees.

"What do I do?" I ask, hoping she actually does have answers that might help, because in this moment, I'm absolutely clueless.

"How do you feel about him?"

"Who?"

"Christian."

"I don't know …" I reply honestly.

"Then I think you need to start with figuring that out," she recommends.

I finally stop my pacing and sit down on the edge of the bed. I don't look at her when I ask. I'm afraid of what else she might see. "Do you think it's possible to be in love with more than one person at the same time?"

She's quiet at first, considering my question thoughtfully. "I think a person can love more than once in his or her life. I don't think your heart can be divided equally between two people at the same time, though. There is always one you'd rather be with, one you think about when you're away from them, one who makes life its best when they're with you."

I look at her. "I think that's Henry."

"You need to know it's him," she urges. She opens her arms, and I fall onto her shoulder, letting her warmth wrap around me. Sighing deeply, I know she's right, but I just don't know how to be sure.

"Have you talked to Henry lately?" she asks me.

I don't move, content in my friend's embrace. "Yeah, I think he can sense something."

"What makes you say that?"

"He seems standoffish. Honestly, it's been weird between us since he went home," I explain.

"Why do you think that is?" she asks.

"I wish I knew. I keep thinking I should just get on a plane and head back home." She's quiet, and I'm surprised my revelation didn't provoke a reaction. "Is that what you think I should do? Fly home?"

"Do you really want me to answer that?" she questions.

I sit up and turn to look at her. "I wouldn't have asked if I didn't want you to answer."

"If you want to marry Henry, you probably should go home," she answers cryptically.

"That isn't any kind of answer at all," I snap.

"I can't tell you what to do, and if that's what you're looking for, it's not going to happen."

"So you think if I stay I'll end up with Christian?"

"I didn't say that."

"No—you're not saying anything," I huff. I watch as she stands and walks to the window. She peers out, something haunting her. "You clearly have something to say. Why don't you just say it?"

She turns; the look in her eyes is filled with pain. She doesn't want to have this conversation.

"What's wrong with you?" I demand.

"You don't want me tell you, trust me," she groans.

"Please, just tell me why you're being so weird."

"Paige, Christian loves you."

"I know, he keeps telling me that. What's your point?"

"He's back. He's him again. Olivia has her uncle, and Colin finally has his brother back. I just don't want things not to work out and—" She stops herself, starting to fidget, refusing to make eye contact.

"You don't want me to mess him up again," I snap, her apprehension suddenly obvious.

"I didn't say that," she quickly defends.

"You didn't have to, I can see it all over your face."

"No, that's not it. It's just—"

"Say it!" I demand.

She shifts her gaze up to mine, bites her lips, and with a deep breath she tells me, "If you have no intention of leaving Henry, then you should probably stop this now. Maybe you should go home."

"Hey, what's going on up here?" I hear Colin's voice, right before he enters the room.

"Oh," Emmie quickly says, scurrying across the room to wrap her arms around her husband. "Nothing, we were just talking about what Paige has planned for the day."

Colin's eyes shift between us. He can see that something is going on between us, but he can't seem to figure it out. "Okay—well I just wanted to let Paige know she has a visitor in the gallery."

"I do?" I ask, pressing my lips together curiously.

"It's Christian," he explains.

"Oh," I say, nodding. "Can you let him know I'll be right down?"

"Sure," Colin says, turning to exit. He hesitates, turns back and looks at us. "Are you sure everything's okay in here?"

Emmie and I both nod.

"Things are fine, go tell Christian she'll be right down," Emmie instructs, practically shoving him out of the room. She wastes no time once he's gone. She turns and walks straight over to me.

"Hey, come here." She reaches out, and I stand and face her.

"What?" I groan, still annoyed only moments ago she told me to go back to New York.

"Listen, I love you like a sister. Christian is my brother now, and I'd love nothing more than the two of you to get back together. If there's a chance, I say go for it. All I'm saying is, if you've made up your mind, and you'll be marrying Henry no matter what, stop this now."

"Maybe I should tell Henry about the three dates."

"If you tell him, there's a good chance he'll call off the wedding. Are you prepared for that outcome?" Emmie asks.

I shake my head.

"Then I say you wait. Just promise me, if you keep going down this path, you'll be as gentle as you can with Christian. We can't lose him again."

"I promise," I agree. It is hard to be upset with Emmie for being protective of Colin's brother. Her loyalty is amazing. I know this.

"You better go see what he wants," she adds, then hugs me tightly.

I RACE DOWN the stairs still distracted by the conversation I'd just had with Emmie. So distracted, in fact, I don't notice I am wearing sweatpants and an over-sized t-shirt still. When I duck through the curtain into the gallery, I don't see Christian right away. Moving into the room a few steps, he comes into view, standing at one of the side windows peering out.

Emmie's words keep going through my mind. Maybe she is right, I still have every intention of marrying Henry. Perhaps it is time I put an end to this charade.

As I watch him silently, he lifts a hand, running his fingers through his raven hair. The strands fall perfectly into place, framing his face. I take a deep breath, letting him know I'm there. I'm in awe of the way he looks as the sun shines in on the bridge of his nose. He turns and smiles at me, but I'm not looking at his smile.

My eyes wander to his body, his strong forearm flexes as he holds something on the other side of his body, out of my sight. I'd always thought his lips were the picture of perfection, and now I am even more convinced as I peer at them, now slightly parted. The top lip always lifts higher on the right side, but the crookedness is part of his charm.

"I like it," he says, without a formal greeting. I glare, puzzled, but then see his gaze focused on my outfit.

I shrug. "Casual Saturdays, what's up?" I want to delay the talk I know needs to be had.

Moving around to one side, Christian pulls an antique wooden body form from behind him. "You took off so fast last night I didn't have a chance to give you the surprise I'd gotten for you."

"What?" I gasp in disbelief, scurrying across the cool concrete floors in my bare feet, to run my hands along the form. "Where did you get this? It's amazing."

"I spotted it at the flea market I went to in Austin last week. As soon as I saw it, I thought of you."

"Oh my God, look at this thing, it's gorgeous."

"Yeah," he continues, and with a couple flips and turns of a mechanism hidden in the rear of the mannequin he proceeds to show me the magic that hides within it. "You can adjust hip and waist size with these parts right here."

"Get out!" I exclaim, slapping his arm with the back of my hand.

"I take it you like it then?" he asks, his face eager with anticipation.

I smile. It is so thoughtful, but how am I going to tell him that our first date was now our last date as well. "I love it, thank you."

I reach a hand to shake his. He looks at the extended limb and chuckles, but shakes it nonetheless. It feels as awkward as I thought it would.

"I had a really good time last night," he adds.

"I did too," I answer honestly. "Dinner was incredible. Thanks for that."

"What is that?" I hear Emmie's voice behind me.

"Can you believe this thing?" I say, turning around and showing off my new treasure. "Christian found it at the flea market in Austin. Oh! How much do I owe you?"

"It's on me," he insists.

"No, please, let me pay you for it," I say firmly.

"Paige, please, I wanted you to have it." The sincerity is heavy in his tone.

"You have to at least let me buy you dinner or something," I offer, suddenly realizing that I pretty much just asked him out on a date.

"Actually, I planned on going bowling later tonight, so how about you buy the first game," he suggests.

"It's a deal," I agree gladly, the arrangement much less threatening than dinner alone with him.

"Bowling!" Emmie exclaims, "I want to go. Colin, hey, Colin—come here."

I giggle at the sheer panic on Christian's face as his sister-in-law invites herself along on his private time with me.

"What is it, hon?" Colin asks, entering the room, Olivia bouncing on his hip.

"Do you think the Carters will babysit tonight?" Emmie inquires.

"I don't know. That's awfully short notice," Christian interjects.

"I don't know—probably, why?" Colin replies, ignoring his brother's opinion.

"We're going bowling with Paige and Christian!" she exclaims, patting her beloved on the ass.

"Sounds fun, I'll call them," Colin says, before tossing Olivia up into the air repeatedly.

"Great," Christian moans. "I guess I'll see *all* of you tonight."

Just before the front door closes behind him, I call after, saying, "It's a date then."

I can see he wants to say something else, but it is too

late. The door closes, and I manage to make our second date a harmless double with my best friend. Maybe I will be able to get through these three dates without anyone getting hurt.

~

CHAPTER 19

*C*HRISTIAN HAD ASKED for Emmie and Colin to meet us at the bowling alley, but the more time I spend alone with him, the more danger I'm in for something inappropriate transpiring between us. Without a word to him, I tell Emmie we should all ride together; she's thrilled by the idea. However, Christian looks a little clueless when everyone piles into his truck without explanation.

Driving down the old highway that leads to the local bowling alley, Colin kicks into story mode. One of the great things about being friends with brothers, is that even if one of them likes to hide his embarrassing stories from you, the other one is always eager to share.

Colin reveals that soon after moving to Bastrop, Christian had to purchase a new vehicle because he bent the frame of his little Honda when he ran off the road and ended up in a ditch to avoid a deer. Christian's warning when I first arrived, about driving and the deer population in Bastrop, suddenly makes a lot more sense.

When the four of us lived in New York, couples nights were a regular thing for us. We would watch cheesy horror flicks with massive bowls of buttered popcorn, or head down to Kings to watch that night's entertainment. The evening feels so familiar and there is a comfort about it I am happy to embrace.

The small bowling alley is quaint, and it's quickly obvious all of the patrons know one another.

"You're in the lane next to us," Christian informs Colin.

"So, how about we put a friendly little wager on this," Colin suggests, pushing into his brother's space.

"Paige isn't a bowler, so that doesn't seem fair," Christian argues. "How about we get a handicap for her?"

"Hey!" I protest, feeling incredibly insulted.

"Fair enough, ten pins?" Colin agrees.

"Wait a second," I huff.

"Deal," Christian exclaims, offering a hand to shake on the agreement.

Emmie shakes her head, laughing. "Ignore them. Once they start this crap, it's too late."

"If Em and I win, you have to change ten dirty diapers, and I mean number two, buddy," Colin tosses out the wager eagerly.

"Fine, and if we win?" Christian inquires.

"What do you want?" Colin asks cautiously.

"You owe me ten hours of free labor."

"That doesn't seem equal," I interject.

"Have you smelled Olivia's diapers?" Colin questions before enthusiastically agreeing. "Deal!"

The game goes pretty much how everyone expected.

Christian and I trail at least five to ten pins at all times, even with the handicap. Though Christian and Colin try their best to relay the useful hints that will help my game, including adjusting my stance approach, release, and even my breathing, nothing seems to help.

However, toward the seventh frame, things begin to shift, and I find my stride. Considering I've been bowling twice in my entire life, and both times were in high school, I don't know how I could suddenly find a stride, but I wasn't about to complain.

"All right babe," Christian says. At first the term unnerves me, then I decide to shake it off. "You can do this. I know you can. Look, Emmie only knocked six pins down on that last one. She'll never pick up those four pins in her next roll. You can get a strike here, I know you can."

"Thanks, Christian," Emmie snaps.

"This is war, no pity missy," Christian taunts back.

Over the speaker system in the bowling alley, the song switches. I turn a bright shade of red as I hear John Hiatt's "Have a Little Faith In Me" echoing across the lanes.

"You hear that?" Christian shouts, wildly waving his arms and jumping around. "The bowling Gods are speaking to you right now! They have faith in you. You can do this!"

I start laughing so hard I have to take a moment to catch my breath.

"Stop," I squeal between puffs of air. "I'm going to pee my pants."

"Oh no, peeing on the alley is grounds for immediate disqualification. We win!" Colin exclaims.

Christian kneels down, looking me in the eyes. "Are

you going to let him talk to you like that? Are you going to let these jokers win? Or are you going to show them just what a city girl can do?"

"Yeah, that's right!" I shout. "I can do this."

Blocking out all of the noise surrounding me, including the shouts coming from Colin as he attempts to get in my head, I prepare myself. The only thing standing between victory and me are those ten pins, staring at me, taunting me from the end of the lane. Those bitches are going down.

I close my eyes and try to recall all of the instruction Christian has given me. Middle finger, ring finger, and thumb in holes—check; four to five even steps as I approach, stay low, good knee bend, make sure of a stable follow through, and release. Release, damn it! The ball makes a loud popping noise as the suction around my thumb suddenly releases, the ball now at eye level.

I flinch, drawing my arms and head into my chest, preparing for the loud thud as the ball connects with alleyway. I can't look up, I don't want to see the descent, which in my mind, I have made peace with the fact this most certainly must end in a gutter-ball.

As I turn and see Christian's expression, he fist pumps crazily in the air, and I realize things are not as I assume. Spinning around, I watch, everything seems to be moving in slow motion. I hold my breath as my ball crashes into the pins, sending them flying in all directions. I gasp in disbelief as one pin rockets into the lane next to us, knocking down the four standing pins from Emmie's last roll.

I scream, turning to look at all of my friends' faces.

They aren't shouting as I expect; instead, they are all staring, their bottom jaws hanging low.

"So does that mean I get fourteen?" I ask before delivering a wide and satisfied grin.

The utter shock quickly fades into riotous laughter and yelling. "We're not worthy," Colin repeats, acting as though he is bowing down to me.

"I say they automatically win, for that move," Emmie suggests.

"Hey woman, ten poop-filled diapers are on the line here," Colin reminds her.

"True," she replies quickly, hopping to her feet and rubbing Colin's shoulders, giving him a pep talk. "Are you going to let them take this away from us, babe? I know you can do this, you're Colin Bennett. You're the best at everything you do."

"Yeah! That's right," Colin says before beginning to woof as if he were a dog.

"That was amazing," Christian praises me.

"I know, and now I need to head to the little girl's room," I reply, racing up the stairs without a moment's hesitation.

When I return, everyone is patiently waiting and watching. Emmie has already taken her turn, as well, and things are looking grim for her and Colin with only three pins knocked down.

"What happened?" I ask, walking into the pit area, looking at Emmie.

"Why don't you ask Christian?" Emmie huffs, crossing her arms playfully.

"Hey, it's not my fault you're so easily distracted."

"He kept chanting 'choke' when it was my turn."

"Christian!" I scorn.

He looks at me, lowering his eyebrows. "Ten, we're talking about ten stank-ass diapers."

I laugh, walking past my friends and rolling the ball, this turn much less epic and with a total of four pins. The game continues in such a way for the next couple frames. Ultimately, my strike is enough to clench the win, but by only a few pins.

"Sorry honey," Emmie says, running her fingers through Colin's shaggy hair.

"We were so close," he grumbles. "I should have never agreed to the handicap."

It's such a fun evening, and I'm sad to see it come to an end, but much to my delight, the rest of the crew feels the same way, and we head home for pie. It is a beautiful night, with incredible friends, and my heart feels full, at least until Christian gets me alone.

"Can I talk to you for a second?" he asks, stepping off to the side.

"Sure," I reply hesitantly.

"Yeah, umm—I wanted to tell you I had a lot of fun tonight," he begins.

"I did too," I reply, but I can tell something is bothering him. "Are you okay?"

He looks at the floor, before his eyes begin shifting nervously around the room. "Not exactly," he says at last.

"What's wrong?" I question, now deeply concerned.

"I'm leaving." His reply confuses me. I stand there in silence, trying to process what he means. "I got a job in Dallas."

"What do you mean you got a job?" I attempt to clarify.

"You know, an order. It's a referral from that last big rush I did. They need me to help with a hand-carved stairwell banister for a home there, so I'll need to do it on site."

"Oh, okay. Why are you telling me this?"

He seems slightly annoyed and insulted by my question. "I'll be gone for a couple weeks."

"I go home in a couple weeks," I remind him.

"I know, but we have one more date," he adds.

"What?"

"You promised me three dates," he repeats.

"I have to go home; I need to be there for my show. I'm sorry, I can't help that you took on a job out of town," I explain, slightly relieved we won't have to go through any further charades.

"I'll work through the night to get it done faster, and I'll be home in ten days. Promise me you won't leave before I get back," he begs.

"I can't," I say, knowing full well I can give him those two weeks.

"Please, I wouldn't take the job except this guy is important for another one of my projects."

I consider saying no, but with Christian gone for two weeks, I know I'll have a lot of focus time to finish up the details. "I can stay the two weeks, but then I have to go."

"Fair enough," he says, a slight smile on his face. "Thank you."

I nod in response. And that is it; by the time I wake in the morning, he has already left for Dallas.

CHAPTER 20

*R*UNNING MY FINGERS across the garment in my hands, I take a deep breath. That's it; it's done. My entire show is ready for the runway. I even managed to create the two alternate pieces I was certain I wouldn't have time for.

Standing up and walking to the other side of the room, I place the dress on a hanger and slip it into the shipping box, before taping it shut. Anxiety floods over me again, my heart nervously fluttering for a moment. The idea of shipping a box of my garments—garments I've spent months working so tirelessly on—is a little overwhelming.

I take a deep breath, then push out all of the air from my lungs. I move on to another box along the wall. Pressing a couple stray fabric samples inside, I tape it shut. The last couple days have been a whirlwind. Part of preparing to return to New York, means shipping back all of the supplies we brought here. I've certainly rethought Henry's suggestion about hiring a personal assistant.

Damn it, focus, Paige! I've been telling myself that for over a week now. It seems like I do anything but focus. For the past couple days, every time I call Henry, he either doesn't answer, or is about to head off to some meeting and has no time to talk to me. Things feel unnatural, to say the least. I can't figure out if it's him, or if somehow I might be at the root of the issue.

Then there's Christian, who, no matter how many times I tell myself not to think about him, in the end my thoughts seem to always end up settling on him.

"Hello?" Emmie's voice calls out as the sound of the door opening fills the room. "Hey sweetie, how's it going?"

"I feel like I'm drowning in boxes," I reply honestly, looking around at the massive amount of work ahead of me. "But, on a positive note, I finished that last dress, and the entire show is boxed up and ready to go."

"That's awesome!" Emmie exclaims as she crosses the room to give me the awkward sideways squeeze-hug.

"Yeah, but now I have to start packing up all the other stuff to ship back. God, how in the hell did Henry get all of this stuff down to me? It must have taken him forever," I remark.

"Well, I'm here to help. And then Colin can head over later and carry the boxes to the post office for us."

"Are you serious?" I ask, thrilled at the offer.

"Of course, you've helped us so much over the past couple months between Olivia and the gallery, it's the least we can do," Emmie insists, immediately digging in and placing items from the work table in a nearby discarded box.

"You do realize you were the one who opened up your home to me and who has been feeding me every night since I got here," I remind her.

"And you'd do exactly the same for us," she replies. We both continue our work in silence until she asks, "Is Henry excited about you coming home?"

I mull over the question in my mind for a few seconds. Had she asked me only weeks ago, the answer would have been a resounding yes, but honestly I just didn't know what was going on in his head anymore. "I suppose."

"You suppose?" Emmie parrots, then laughs. "What's with the melancholy? I thought all you could think about was going home."

"It was. I do, I mean—" I stammer. "I don't know. After Thanksgiving I was so sure about where I was and where Henry and I were, but now, every thing just seems screwed up."

"What are you talking about?" she asks, setting down the scissors in her hand and walking over to face me.

I shake my head. "I just feel ... confused."

"Wait." Emmie gives me her *I'm-gonna-nail-you-with-tough-questions look*. "Is this about Christian?"

"No!" I exclaim. "I—maybe. I don't know."

"Paige, what's going on? When Christian left for Dallas you told me you were still certain you were going to marry Henry."

"And I am."

"Are you?"

"Jesus," I huff, collapsing back onto a stiff metal chair. "See what I mean about everything being screwed up?"

"Do you have feelings for Christian?"

"I don't know, maybe. Since he's been gone I keep thinking about him. Why am I thinking about him?"

"Thinking about him how?" she pushes.

"All kinds of crap. At first I was upset. I don't even know if upset's the right word … annoyed, maybe. He pushes me to have these dates with him and explore my feelings, but then he turns around, and just before I head back to New York to marry another man, he leaves." Retelling my frustration only seems to stir the feelings in me once more.

"I know it's hard to understand, but Christian has been trying to get that contact for at least six months. The guy's really important for plans he has."

"But I'm not important?" I inquire.

"If you weren't important he wouldn't be rushing back early," Emmie points out.

"How come every man I choose puts his career before me?" I ask, throwing my head back and huffing.

"That's not fair, seeing as you haven't chosen Christian; it's not like you're his girlfriend. And I thought Henry always put you first?"

"He does, I guess. It just seems like since I got back from Europe he's always at the office."

"You were barely home before you came down here, and I believe that was for your own career goals." Damn it, she always has a way of putting the straight truth on me. I love her and hate her for it.

"You're right," I concede. "I think I'm looking for things to be pissed about when I'm really just pissed off at myself."

"Why?" Emmie now seems as confused as I feel.

"I love Henry. I should have never agreed to those dates. All it did was confuse the situation."

"Christian will be home tonight," Emmie says. But I already know this information. I think that is why all of my emotions were coming to a head. "What are you going to do? He's expecting that third date."

"I don't know."

"I think you do. Maybe you don't want to admit it. What's your gut telling you to do?"

I close my eyes, clear my thoughts, and speak the first words that come to mind, "Marry Henry."

When my eyelids lift, and I peer over at my friend, she looks a little sad. She always tells me to follow my heart, but it's obvious my heart doesn't align with her goals.

"Then you need to tell him tonight." Her words are soft and gentle. I know she's right. I nod, and we go back to work, making small talk about Colin and Olivia, and eventually, the wedding.

CHAPTER 21

A DAY I hoped would drag on for an eternity flies by. After Emmie helped me reach the decision about what needed to happen with Christian, I block him from my thoughts. I spend the rest of the day working along side my best friend.

I laugh harder than I've laughed in years as Emmie and I share funny stories of our time together as roommates in New York. Some of the things didn't seem funny when we were living them, but looking back, they are absolutely hilarious.

One of my favorites is the story about William Stryker. Emmie had met this guy in a park, at the time she thought the meeting was just random, and had no clue he was a private investigator hired by her late husband's father. After bumping into her, and some heavy flirting, she had agreed to go out on a date with him.

It had been perhaps the worst date of all time. To hear Emmie retell the events from her perspective put an entirely new level of hysteria on it. Em is nice enough to add special effects and voice over impressions of me at the part where I attempted to intervene, threatening this perv with bodily harm. In that moment, I wish I could put her in my pocket and take her back to New York with me. However, I'm relieved she'll be heading to New York soon after I return and will be staying with me until the wedding.

The evening air is actually quite cool, and I decide to go with jeans, riding boots, a long sleeve, form-fitting black t-shirt, and oversized gray cardigan for my date with Christian. I consider canceling, but then decide it's only fair for me to share my intentions of following through on my marriage to Henry, in person. It seems like the least I can do, seeing as I agreed to this craziness in the first place.

"Paige, Christian's here," I hear Emmie's voice carry up the staircase. I click the top button on my phone and glance down for the time. Eight o'clock on the nose. Apparently, punctuality is also something new and improved about Christian Bennett.

I stare at my reflection for a moment longer, then with a deep breath, I turn and make my way out of the room and down into the kitchen, where Emmie, Colin, Olivia, and Christian are all standing. Everyone stops and stares at me. I suddenly feel very self-conscious.

"You look incredible," Christian says, smiling. I notice he's wearing blue jeans and a button-up plaid shirt. I sigh a breath of relief to know I'm not underdressed for the evening's plans.

"Thanks, shall we go?" I ask immediately. I want this

date to get started, so I can let Christian down gently, and then finally be able to move on with my life.

"Oh— sure," he says, a little surprised by my forwardness.

"You kids have fun," Colin says is his best elderly voice, waving to us as we walk out the door. From the corner of my eye, I see Emmie give her husband a swift elbow to his ribs. They really are cute—almost annoyingly so.

"Everything okay?" Christian asks as we approach his truck. He opens the passenger door, awaiting my answer.

"Yeah, why wouldn't it be?"

"Seemed like you wanted a quick exit back there. I wanted to make sure you were okay."

"I don't know, I guess I'm just eager to get this show on the road," I reply, climbing into the truck.

"Missed me that much, huh?" he says and then closes the door before I have a chance to reply.

He walks around and climbs into the driver's side. I decide to attempt small talk. "So how was your trip?"

He smiles. "Really good, but I missed you like crazy."

At his admission, I can feel the butterflies start in the pit of my stomach. *Focus Paige, you're going back to New York, and you're going to marry Henry.*

"Wow, nothing, huh?" Christian jokes, apparently surprised his comment doesn't elicit more of a reaction. Knowing it will only encourage his persistence if he has any indication I might be struggling with our current circumstances, I don't take the bait.

"Did you get what you wanted out of the trip?" I continue.

Christian looks at me, examining my face, but I simply

stare straight ahead, watching the yellow road lines coming at us, one two-foot dash at a time.

"Something seems off, are you sure everything is okay?" he asks me again.

I laugh, trying to convince him that he is being silly for even asking. "Of course. I just wanted to know if you got what you wanted out of your trip."

Christian furrows his brow, and then his expression shifts into one of acceptance. "Actually, I think the guy's going to be able to help me out."

"Oh really?" I prod, hoping to talk about anything except the hope he has of a possible relationship resuming between us.

"Yeah." There's excitement in his voice as he talks to me. "He was really impressed with the work I did for him, and he said he'd like to come and take a look at my project after New Year's and see if he can help out."

"What project?" I ask, realizing nobody has given me details about this big important thing Christian is working on.

"You'll soon find out," he taunts.

"What? Where are we going?" I inquire. I'd assumed we would be grabbing a bite to eat at Roadhouse, but it just registers that he didn't take the turn he needed to a half-mile back. We're going somewhere else, but where I don't know.

"It's a surprise."

I'm starting to get frustrated. I planned on a quick dinner, letting him down gently, and being in bed early tonight. "No, please, no surprises tonight. I'm exhausted. I worked all day long, and I thought we were just going on a simple date."

Christian doesn't look at me—just stares straight ahead. We begin to slow, our headlights pulling to the left-hand side of the road. At last, they shine onto a gravel drive, and Christian breaks his silence. "I'm sorry, I didn't realize you'd be so tired. This is our last date, and since there's a good chance you'll be going back to New York for good, I wanted it to be special."

Did he just say what I think he said? Perhaps Christian is starting to come to his senses. Maybe he realizes there's no chance I'm ever going to leave Henry for him.

"I don't understand, where are we going?" I ask.

He seems nervous. I have no idea where he could possibly be taking me. I look out the right window; the landscape is shifting, the trees increasing in density all around us.

"I thought it might be nice to have a picnic," he says.

"At night?" I ask, staring at him, and then looking around again. "In the forest?"

"Eh— not exactly," he begins. "Well, at night, and technically in a forest, but I like to think of it as a castle in a forest."

"Christian!" I blurt out, frustrated by the lack of a straight answer. "What cast—" But before I can finish my thought, he rounds a corner, and a building comes into focus. At least what looks like it can be a building, eventually—a large portion still appears to be a shell.

When the headlights reposition to the front of the structure, I see plenty of construction gear come into focus, stones stacked to the left, and pallets of wood that are covered with tarps to the right.

"Welcome to my home sweet home," he says. I sit there, speechless and confused. "Or at least it will be, if I can ever finish the damn place."

"Wait, what?" I gasp. "You're building this?"

"Every piece from scratch," he boasts proudly.

I look back and stare at the structure. To the left are windows that reach from floor to ceiling, and extend all the way down the wall, leading to two oversized wooden doors. It's obvious the doors have some sort of pattern carved into them, but I'm too far away to make it out.

"I can't believe this."

"Well, I guess I can't say just me. Colin helps whenever he has spare time, and deals like the one I was trying to make in Dallas will help a lot," he continues.

"What deal?" I ask, not waiting for him, but opening the passenger door, stepping out onto the drive, taking in the insane amount of detail around me.

"I need massive steel beams brought in, and one set into that giant oak tree back there for support."

I squint, trying to see what he is talking about, the dark shielding my vision somewhat. Then it becomes clear. "Is the house built around that tree?"

"Yeah it is, pretty cool, right," Christian says, barely able to contain his excitement. "But when we started working on the roof we discovered some logistics about the tree expanding. So I need to build an atrium around the tree in order to allow room for the trunk to expand through the years. I had to have a structural engineer come out, and it set the project way back. Everything seems to be getting back on track though."

"This place is incredible." I remark, walking up the flagstone steps.

"I thought you'd like it."

"I can't believe you never told me about it. I've been here for two months," I mutter, reaching down and touching the stone steps as I walk by.

"I was nervous."

"What on Earth would you have to be nervous about?"

"I was afraid you wouldn't like it. It's important to me that you do." There's so much about his statement that frightens me. I decide to change the subject.

Climbing up to the front door, I stop and turn to look at him. He's staring at me with a huge grin across his face. I feel my cheeks flush hot. "It's so big. Won't you get lonely all by yourself?"

"I didn't build it for myself," he answers, moving past me, and turning the knob to the large wooden door before pushing it open. As I take a step forward, the timer on the headlights clicks off, and I lose my footing in the darkness. Reaching out, I grab Christian's arm and steady myself.

"Then who did you build it for?" I inquire. "An investment?"

He shakes his head, "I guess, in a way. One day, I hope to raise my family here." The idea of him creating a family with another woman makes my chest ache, though I know a family is something he wants. "Here, hold onto the wall, and let me get the lights."

Reaching out a hand and placing an open palm on the cool wall, I stand, waiting for the room to be illuminated.

"I wish I could see this place in the daylight," I comment.

Christian doesn't say a word; I can hear him fiddling with something in the corner. And in a second, the room comes to life before my eyes. A warm yellow strand of bulbs is strung back and forth throughout the room, across the large wooden rafters over our heads. A second later I hear Weezer start playing from a speaker in the corner. Instinctively, my hand shifts to my wrist, and I run my fingers over the tattoo of lyrics. He sees me.

"Does it bother him you have that?" he asks.

"He just thinks it's an inspirational tattoo, but he doesn't know the story behind it," I explain.

"Why didn't you tell him?" Christian asks me pointedly.

"I didn't want him to hate something on my body. If he knew the story behind the tattoos, it would change the way he saw it."

"It doesn't seem right to lie to the one you love." I'm annoyed by the judgment in his statement.

"I'm not lying," I argue. "The story isn't relevant to my life anymore, so I don't really see any reason to share it." I can see my statement hurts him, and I wonder if I was too harsh.

"I don't know, still seems like a lie," he says, shrugging his shoulders.

I decide I'm not going to get drawn into a conversation about my relationship with Henry. Our dysfunction was none of Christian's business. "What is this?" I ask, my stare shifting to a blanket spread across the floor, a basket off to one side.

"I told you I made us a picnic," he replies, walking over to where I still cling to the wall. Taking my hand, he leads me to the blanket, our flesh touching causing butterflies to erupt in my stomach.

"Are you serious?" I question, and I begin to laugh, trying my best to ignore my body's response to him.

"All right, I'm not sure if laughing is good or bad …" he responds, examining my expression. "Should I be insulted?"

"No!" I gasp. "Oh God—no, this is crazy. I mean crazy good. I can't believe you went to so much trouble, I'm blown away."

"Good, my plan is working then," he chimes before rubbing his hands together in a devilish way.

Flopping down onto the blanket, I prop up on my knees and reach for the basket, welcoming any distraction from his adorableness. Grabbing the wicker box and pulling it close, I glance at him as he sits and ask, "May I?"

"Please do," he replies, waving at me to continue.

Tossing back the lid and digging into the dark cavern, I begin pulling out the hidden treats. Christian narrates the reveal as I go. First there's a tray of various cheeses. I recognize the Brie, and I can smell smoked Gouda, but the others are a mystery. Reaching back in, I find crackers with a choice of fig jam or apple butter.

The next item I pull out confuses me. It appears to be a lighter of some kind. "Umm, what's this?"

He pushes up onto his knees, snatching the device out of my hand, then reaches into the basket and pulls out a container with two white ramekins in it. "It's a torch for dessert."

"Did you make crème brûlée?" I gasp in disbelief.

"Maybe," he says slyly.

"This is too much!" I exclaim, popping a cracker into my mouth.

"Sparkling cider?" he offers, leaning to the side and coming back up with a bottle.

"Yes, please," I answer eagerly. I watch him pop the top and pour the grape cider into plastic cups. As he hands me one, I'm a little overwhelmed by the thoughtfulness of the evening.

Christian lifts his plastic cup into the air and says, "To new beginnings."

"To new beginnings," I agree with a smile, and crash my cup into his, though I know his toast is intended in a different way than my own.

He takes a gulp then lies on his side, propping up his head with an open palm, staring at me as I take a drink. I feel the need to shift the attention.

"You at least have to get a dog."

"Oh, for sure, it wouldn't be a home without a dog."

"So what kind of dog are you getting?"

"What kind would you like us to have?" he asks, lifting his eyebrows as he peers up at me.

"You don't quit, do you?" I shove him gently, causing him to roll over onto his back, us both now snickering.

He sits up, and looking intensely into my eyes says, "Not when it's something I really want."

"Wow, way to make the mood all heavy," I groan.

"Sorry," he mutters, turning and pulling back a corner

of the blanket where he had a small box hidden. "Okay, let's see if I can lighten the mood ... gift time."

"What?" I question, completely perplexed by what's happening.

"Christmas is in a couple weeks, and you're headed back to New York, so I wanted to make sure you got your gift from me."

"I didn't get you anything," I protest.

"I have an idea of something you can give me," he growls, leaning in close.

"I bet you do," I scoff.

"That's later, but right now, open," he commands, placing the box on my lap. I run my hands across the top, glancing up at him and smiling in anticipation. I know I shouldn't be excited, but I am. I know it's probably unwise to even open it, but I can't help myself.

"Well, go on, open it," he pushes me again.

I lift the lid with my eyes closed, and set it to the side. Through squinted vision, I see a book. Opening my eyes, I allow the gift to come into focus. It's a photo album. I have the urge to look at Christian, but I resist. I flip the large red leather cover and look at the first page. Staring back at me is an image of Colin, Christian, and me. I remember the day. It was the end of the summer, and Christian and I were getting ready to start back to high school. Colin took us on a white water rafting trip. It was one of the few vacations I had during my childhood.

"Oh Christian," I gasp.

"You remember that trip? Colin and I had you convinced a bear was going to come in our camp if you didn't pee all around your tent."

"Jesus! I forgot about that. You guys have always been dicks, haven't you?" I laugh; he seems rather pleased with my reaction.

I turn the page, each one holding a whole new set of memories. Our prom, concerts, parties, my first modeling job that he came and cheered me on at, graduation, all of the renovation projects I helped them on. Christian was spinning story after story, each one more passionate and detailed than the previous.

I don't speak as I look through the pages—I simply remember—and it's like a warm blanket being wrapped around me. Before I know what's happening, I feel a surge of tears fill my eyes, and they come spilling out and flooding down my cheeks. *What the hell is this? I don't cry— ever. At least the old Paige didn't.*

At first it's clear Christian doesn't notice my silent crying. But then, it's hard to miss when the drops fall onto the pages of the album.

"Paige?" he questions, scrambling upright and moving in close. "What's wrong?" I can't answer him; I don't know what to say. "Did I do something?"

"No," I reply through snotty sniffles. "You're perfect."

"Then what's wrong?" he pushes deeper.

"I don't know, nothing—" I start. "Everything." Setting the photo album off to one side, I rub my legs briskly, the heatless structure starting to numb my extremities in the cool evening air.

"Are you cold?" he asks, noticing my body language. I nod, pulling my knees up to my chest.

He wastes no time, hopping to his feet, and crossing the oversized living room, he kneels down in front of the fireplace. "All right, I haven't lit this up since we tested it, so sorry if it smells a little funky at first," he warns me, then moments later I watch as the starter log lights up, its flames tickling the wooden hunks Christian placed on top of it.

"Thank you," I mutter.

Moving to the speaker, he turns the music down, and flips off the light strands over our heads. The quiet and calmness of the dark, with just the orange glow of the fire, is actually quite nice. I take a deep breath, trying to figure out what exactly sent me into my frenzy.

In a second, he's back at my side, moving in close. He reaches out to put an arm around me, but then hesitates, and looks to me for my approval. I should say no, but I can't. I want him to hold me right now, more than anything else in the world. And then he does. His large muscular arm wraps around me.

"Are you going to tell me what's bothering you?" Christian prods.

I shrug my shoulders. I don't want to talk. Pulling away slightly, I lay my head on his lap, and his fingertips graze my temple as he pulls my hair from my face and begins stroking my head. I moan, and then close my eyes.

OPENING MY EYES, I realize morning is here. I feel a body pressed up against me and quickly realize it's Christian. We must have fallen asleep here last night. His arm is draped across my waist. My back is killing me after sleeping on the floor all night, but I don't move. If I move, I know he'll wake up. If he wakes up, he'll move, too, and then this moment will be over forever.

I try to shift ever so slightly, as I realize I can no longer feel the arm I've fallen asleep on. Even holding my breath doesn't help, Christian stirs as soon as I free my pinned arm. I close my eyes and wonder if he knows that I'm awake as well.

"Paige?" he says as he sits up. "Good morning."

Now that he's up, there's no reason for me to pretend. I sit and try to comb my fingers through my hair. "Morning," I mutter.

He looks around and sees that it's daylight. "We must have fallen asleep last night."

"Yeah, must have. Well, we better get going," I say, rising up onto my knees. But, before I can stand, he grabs my arm and pulls me back down onto my bottom.

He looks into my eyes. "We need to finish our talk."

"I'm sorry?" I play ignorant.

"From last night," he adds.

"I don't know what you're talking about."

He shakes his head. "We're not leaving until you tell me why you were crying."

I collapse the rest of the way onto the blanket. I know even less now than I did then about why I broke down. How can I make him understand how confused I am? Who knows, maybe it's bridal jitters. "I don't know," I say honestly.

Christian narrows his stare. "I think you probably have a pretty good idea."

I ponder what he says. Deep down, I'd also like to know what made me cry. I swallow hard and decide maybe he can help me find the answers. "I don't know—everything has just felt so messed up lately."

"In what way?"

"Look, I get that you still love me, and obviously I still have some sort of feelings for you, but I also know I love Henry. We fit together really well, and he makes me happy. I think coming down here and stirring up all these feelings was a mistake," I explain, almost as much to myself as to him.

"Okay, that's fair," he begins, thinking through my statement. "And I'm sure you do care a lot for Henry. From everything you've told me he's an amazing guy."

"He is!" I declare.

"No one is saying otherwise."

"I know, but the last couple weeks he's been standoffish, and I think he knows that I'm keeping something from him. I'm just so scared I've messed everything up."

"Is it us you're keeping from him?" I nod. "Why did you keep it from him?"

I look at him with a bit of disgust. "Really? Let's not even go there. You're not going to make this into something it's not. You know you are the who pushed me into this, and there was no way I was going to tell my fiancé that I agreed to such an insane thing."

"Slow down, I'm not trying to blame something on you or trick you. I really want to help figure this out ... for both of us. It worries me when you tell me he's changed lately."

"Honestly, I think I've been feeling so guilty he can tell something is up. It's probably my fault."

"I don't understand, we haven't done anything," Christian reminds me.

"Just because we're not screwing around doesn't mean I haven't cheated. Emotional cheating might be worse," I grumble remorsefully.

"So what you're trying to tell me is that you've been carrying on an emotional affair with me?" Christian asks with a half smile.

"You know what I mean."

"No, I don't. You see," he says, moving in close to me. With each word he speaks, he inches even closer to my face. "I know what this is. I know what I want, and I don't have someone else. I don't want someone else. All I want is you. All I've *ever* wanted is you."

"Christian, don't," I say, pushing his body away with my open palms, my stomach flipping in response to his words.

"If you can honestly say that you don't love me, then get up and leave this house right now, but if there is still love for me in your heart, then please, don't give up on us." His voice shakes as he speaks.

"Damn it!" I exclaim, slipping out of his grasp and hopping to my feet. "I'm engaged!"

He quickly follows my lead and stands, rushing up and grabbing me by my upper arms. "But you shouldn't be marrying him—you should be marrying me."

I know he's about to kiss me. I can see it in his eyes. He can see that I know it, and when I don't pull away, he knows I want him to as much as he wants to. Pulling me close with his strong hands, he presses his mouth against mine. My lips part, and his wet, warm tongue glides in, exploring me.

I don't struggle, but instead I lift a hand, placing it on the middle of his back. I lift the other to his head, running my fingertips through his hair. I'm sad when he begins to pull away, but then filled with excitement as I feel him trailing little kisses down my chin, then my neck, then—

"I can't!" I shout, finally managing to push him away.

He looks at me intensely. I can see the raw desire in him, and it's making me want him even more. "You can't what? Marry him or be with me?"

"I can't do this to Henry," I answer.

"You're right, you can't. You need to go home to New York and tell him it's over."

I stand there, silent, processing all of Christian's words, and as much as I want to argue with him, and tell him he's wrong, that Henry is my soul mate, I can't. No matter how much I care for Henry, I know there's a reason I keep getting drawn back into Christian.

"I know," I moan.

Christian looks at me, unsure. "You know what?"

"I can't marry Henry," I say plainly.

"Are you serious?" he asks, as if expecting me to suddenly change my mind.

I nod. Before I can say a word, he scoops me up and spins me around, holding me tightly. It feels like he might never let me go, and deep down, I'm fine with that.

"Wait, please," I plead. He stops spinning, loosens his grasp, and looks at me.

"We have to stop this for now," I explain. With those words he releases me, and steps back. "Wait, just listen. I care for Henry a lot, and the last thing I want to do is to disrespect him any more than I already have. Let me go home and tell him we're over. I'll do the fashion show, and then we can figure out whatever this is between us."

"Whatever you think's best. God, Paige, I love you so much."

"I love you, too," I say softly, finally allowing myself to admit it.

CHAPTER 22

*A*LL I'VE BEEN able to think about since leaving Christian's half-built home in the woods is how on Earth I'm going to tell Henry that we're over. When I tell Emmie what happened, she does her best not to explode with excitement, but it's obvious she approves of this choice much more than my original one of marrying Henry.

She, of course, suggests the straight and honest approach. But I think about that repeatedly, and it seems absurd to tell him I love him, but I love someone else more, and that's why I can't marry him. It isn't like I can tell Henry I don't love him, because damn it, I do. That's why this is hurting so much.

On the plane ride I keep practicing the speech in my head. I don't tell him I'm coming home a day early. Somehow I think the element of surprise might work better, but it isn't making the conversation I'm about to have any easier. On the cab ride to our home, my thoughts shift to the logistics of the break up.

Henry is a practical guy. He works with numbers day in and day out, and I'm certain after the initial shock of the break up, these will be the questions that will arise. I don't know what this new phase of my life will look like though. I'm about to have a runway show, and what if I sell my line to a retailer?

Will Christian want to come to New York? His niece is in Texas. The home he's building for his future family is in Texas. He's putting down roots there. Does that mean I will have to be the one to move? But wait—don't I have roots, too? I might not have family who I'm willing to even speak to in New York, but that's where I was born and raised. It's where I've built my life.

I pay the taxi driver and pull my single carry-on bag from the back seat. Glancing up at the incredibly tall building, I wonder what Henry might be doing at that exact moment. Will I surprise him in the shower? Oh my God, what if he's naked? I am still insanely attracted to Henry. What would happen? I need to stop thinking about such things.

I express my greetings to the doorman, who is elated to see I've returned and tells me he hopes Mr. Wallace is feeling better. The comment seems odd, but I dismiss it and make my way inside and up the elevator.

When you're marrying one of the wealthiest men in the building, it's quite amazing how many people know you. Between the lobby and our apartment, I must run into half a dozen neighbors who want to discuss my recent travels. The problem is, all I want is to be home and get this conversation over with. I'm ready to get off this roller coaster.

At last I'm here, staring at the big red door. On the other side will be Henry. On the other side will be the end to the life I've built with an incredible man. I close my eyes and tell myself, *You're doing the right thing. You love Christian. You can't keep pretending.*

I slide my key into the lock and turn; I open the door and step inside. The place is dark, the curtains are drawn, and there's no sound of running water. He isn't in the shower. I breathe a sigh of relief and set my bag down, closing the door behind me. "Henry?"

There's no answer. Maybe I missed him.

Moving into the dark hallway that leads to our bedroom, I call out his name again, "Henry?"

I hear rustling, and upon pushing open the door, I poke my head in to see him, just starting to stir from a nap. "Henry?" I say softly one last time.

"Paige?" he moans and sits up wiping the sleep from his eyes. I see his bare back, so slender that the bones of his spine are sticking out in an alarming way. I immediately cross the room and look at him. His eyes are sunken.

"Baby," the words slip out of my mouth instinctually. "Are you all right?"

"Yeah, I've just been a little under the weather," he defends and then grabs his robe from the end of the bed, wrapping it around himself. "What are you doing home? I didn't expect you for a couple more days."

I think about the question. I've just walked in; I'm not ready to dive straight into the devastating break up talk.

"I finished my work and decided I wanted to come home early." So far, that is mostly the truth.

He hugs me, kisses my cheek, and leaves the bedroom,

heading into the kitchen, to pour a glass of orange juice. I watch him. He seems different.

"Are you sure everything is okay?" I ask again.

"Of course," he replies, but I don't believe him. "Well …" he hesitates.

"What is it?" I press.

"We need to talk," he answers softly.

My stomach flutters, and I wonder if he somehow knows about Christian already. "Okay."

"It's about the wedding." As he says the words, I feel my stomach drop like an elevator plummeting from the top floor to the basement.

"All right, is something wrong?" I inquire, following Henry over to the small cafe table.

He looks at me. There's a pain in his eyes. He knows something, and while I'm not sure exactly what, I'm confident I see pain. He doesn't respond.

The room is dark, but even without the light I can tell he's pale. "Have you been resting, like the doctors said?"

"Paige," he begins, completely ignoring my inquiry. "This is going to be hard to say, so please, just let me get through it. After you hear me out, we can decide what to do about the wedding."

What to do about the wedding? So he does know something, and he's going to call off the wedding. Why does this bother me? Shouldn't I be glad he's about to do this for me? Say nothing, Paige, just listen.

"Something's happened." I swallow hard at his statement. "I went to the doctor for the elimination diet, and it still wasn't helping, at least not like it should. Two weeks ago I got back the results of my head scan."

This is not how I expect the conversation to go. Where are the accusations, the screaming, and the disgust? My heart races as a panic rushes over me.

"Is everything all right?" I ask, staring closer now at all the things that have changed about his appearance.

"I'm afraid not."

I'm not thinking about the wedding or about Christian any longer. All I can think is this is bad, and everything is about to change forever. "Henry, what's going on?"

He takes a deep breath, leans forward, and scoops my hand into his. I notice how cold he is, and how slender his fingers have become. He looks me in the eyes and softly says, "I have a grade four brain tumor."

"What?" I gasp, shaking my head, not wanting to allow the information to sink in. "No, that's not right."

"It's not good, sweetheart. It's malignant," he continues. I notice he's calm.

"I don't understand," I finally manage to say, my eyes welling up quickly.

"I'm dying," he replies plainly.

"No, that can't be, there has to be some sort of mistake. How bad is it?"

"There's nothing else they can do right now. The tumor is too large for surgery, and because of its stage, it's growing aggressively. They want try and shrink it with chemo in hopes the tumor gets small enough that they'll be able to operate."

"Okay good, so there's a plan. When does the chemo start?" I question, my mind focused completely on the problem and how to fix it.

"That's just it, I'm not sure I'm going to have it."

"What? What do you mean? You have to have it."

"Honey, the doctors say my chances are pretty slim. As it is now, if I get plenty of rest, who knows how long I could live with this." he explains.

"No! You just want to give up? That's not an option!" I exclaim, refusing to accept what he's saying. "Henry, you have to promise me, if there's a chance, even a slim one, then you're going to fight."

"Listen, you need to take a deep breath. I've had time to process this, you haven't."

"Yeah, tell me about it! I can't believe you've known about this for two weeks, and you haven't told me."

"What was I supposed to say? I didn't even know how I felt about it," he explains.

I furrow my brow, my body jerking at the shock of his statement, "You didn't know how you felt about what?"

"Putting you through this."

I huff, "You're not putting me through anything. I'm here because I want to be," I insist. In a moment everything has been turned on its head, and all I can think about is the idea of Henry no longer being in the world. I wish my heart would stop aching.

"I'm giving you an out. You don't have to do this with me. Nobody will blame you. I won't blame you." His voice is tender and sweet.

"Stop. Stop it now!" I snap. I don't have to think about it. The answer pops out immediately. "Don't be ridiculous. This doesn't change a thing. In a week we'll be married, and I'll be by your side the entire time. We're going to beat this—together."

I'm certain the words I spoke are truer than any other

I have ever spoken. Sitting here with Henry, the idea of death stealing him from my world, there is no more confusion. Christian will move on. Here, with Henry, is exactly where I'm supposed to be. And I am ready to make it that way permanently. We'll figure this out.

Suddenly the reality of what I've done comes crashing down. I assumed Henry was pulling away because he sensed something in me, when in fact, he was fighting here, all by himself. I'm sickened as my epic selfishness settles over me.

"Oh God," I moan, collapsing from my chair onto my knees. "I'm so sorry, baby. I'm so sorry," I say over and over. He assumes I am sorry he's sick, but there is so much more I am sorry for.

He doesn't hesitate to get down on his knees with me, wrapping his arms around my convulsing body, attempting to console me. My sobs are heavier as I feel how weak his grasp is.

"Are you sure?" he asks me. "Everyone would understand if this is too much for you."

"Don't ask again," I tell him through tears. "I love you."

"I love you, too, baby," he says with an intense relief in his voice.

It's more than loving him and knowing he loves me. It's exactly as his mother had told me all those years ago: without him in my life, there will be a hole—one that I doubt could ever be filled. I will marry Henry, and we'll fight this, harder than either of us have fought for anything in our lives.

I decide I'll call Christian first thing tomorrow and tell him I've made a mistake—a terrible mistake.

CHAPTER 23

I'VE WAITED MY entire life for this moment. The day where I take all of my designs from the very earliest stages to full execution of pieces that will be worn down the runway. A dream I thought was impossible is now coming true. But it no longer seems to carry any importance for me.

All I can think about is Henry. I keep wondering if I'd never left New York, would I have seen him deteriorating and forced him to see a specialist much sooner? Would a couple of months mean he had more of a chance? While I was in Christian's arms, I should have been here, focusing on Henry and our wedding.

"Paige," I hear Emmie's voice behind me. She flew in to help with the final details of the show and was staying through the week until the wedding was over. "This young lady here is having trouble fitting into the piece set aside for her. You have her marked as wearing midnight haze."

I turn and size up the model; it's obvious she didn't

provide accurate measurements to the agency. "Send her over to Marcy. She has a couple back up pieces we could try." I turn and begin examining the schedule, making sure the order the pieces appear on stage in is complementary, but I still can't concentrate. Trailing after each thought is one about Henry.

"How are you doing?" Emmie asks, moving in next to me.

"I'm great," I lie. "I can't believe Eva lent me Marcy for the night. It's such a huge help." I'd worked under Eva in Paris when she launched her line. Marcy was my replacement, and boy, is she amazing.

"That's not exactly what I meant," Emmie interjects.

"I don't understand, what do you mean then?"

"I get off the plane this morning and when I get to your place, you drop the 'Henry has cancer' bomb on me, and then we come here. What I mean is, how are you holding up?"

I shake my head and smile at my friend. "I'm not going to let myself get down. Henry said that the doctors told him half the battle is keeping a positive attitude. I wish he didn't have to have treatments before our honeymoon, but I guess the sooner they start the better."

"Paige, honey, do you really think it's a good idea to get married right now?" Emmie asks softly, reaching out and touching my arm.

"What? Henry's sick so I should just abandon him?"

"No, and I think you know me well enough to know that's not what I meant. I'm not saying you should end it with him, but when you left Texas last week you told me you were coming home to tell Henry you still loved Christian."

"I was wrong!" I shout, pulling away, and flashing my friend a warning look.

"I'm not trying to upset you. I just don't want you to make any rash decisions."

"That's exactly what I was doing with Christian. I'd been away from Henry for months, we were barely talking, I was lonely, and it gave Christian the opening to work his way in, and make me have doubts."

"Sweetie, all I'm saying is why not postpone the wedding? It might be easier on Henry," Emmie suggests.

"Henry wants to get married as badly as I do. I'm just thankful I didn't do anything with Christian that I can't undo," I explain, doing my best to keep the volume of my voice in check.

"Fine, I care about you and—"

"You promised," I remind her.

"I know—no telling Colin or Christian about Henry's illness. And I won't. If you're sure this's what you really want, and not just because Henry's sick, then I won't say another word about it," Emmie relents.

I take a step forward, firmly grasping my friend's hands with my own, my voice shaking and my eyes burning with tears. "I love Henry and … I don't know, I guess— some part of me still loves Christian. But what I had with Christian is in my past, and that's where it should stay. I knew that the moment Henry told me about the cancer; it was like an elephant was sitting on my chest. I couldn't breathe or think. I need him to be all right, because he's my other half, and I love him. I can't live without him."

"I won't say a word," Emmie repeats in almost a whisper. "You two will get through this."

Emmie opens her arms and pulls me into an embrace. It feels like her arms wrap around me five times, with warmth I so desperately need. An acceptance and understanding that I've been seeking since I told her. A comfort only my best friend can provide.

"It's going to be such a long road. He's been dealing with the headaches for so long he hardly sleeps. I noticed he even has trouble walking sometimes. What am I going to do?"

Emmie squeezes me tighter. "You're going to fight. You're one of the strongest women I've ever known. If anyone can do this, you can."

"Thank you," I whisper, a tear breaking free and running down my cheek.

CHAPTER 24

$\mathcal{L}$ ITTLE GIRLS DREAM about that perfect day, the one when they walk down the aisle and marry their soul mates, their white knights. It's what fairytales are all about. What's never in the fairy tale is finding out the prince has cancer.

Henry's grandmother has taken care of all of the details regarding the big day with impeccable detail. There's a level of elegance and sophistication that would have left any bride awestruck. The flowers are classic with a mixture of lilies and roses. Though I'd planned on designing the bridesmaids dresses myself, I hadn't had time, but luckily Gram came through on those as well. They are a lovely muted gray, and the color reminds me of a sky just before a storm.

The photographer's name is Jane. I requested another company, but apparently when you decide to hide out in the South for a couple months, you get whatever you get. On a positive note, she seems to be highly qualified. As she snaps moments of the girls and me getting ready, it's hard for me to repeatedly gather my lips into a smile. The poor woman has no idea what's happening in my life, and it's impossible for her to understand that the day, which should be the happiest, now has a huge cloud hanging over it.

There are morning pictures in Central Park, the artistic shots in gritty alleyways, and the obligatory chapel images captured. I can see Jane has many more pre-ceremony poses planned, but I simply can't force another toothy, fake grin. Much to Jane's dismay, I inform her that we have enough images with the bride, but she is welcome to continue with the rest of the girls. Considering half my bridesmaids are model friends, they are used to long photo shoots. Based on Emmie's glare, before I duck away, I don't think she is nearly as understanding.

When I excuse myself, I have no idea where to go. I'm dressed in my handmade wedding gown, and popping into a coffee shop alone seems like a bad idea that will invite many unwanted questions. I decide to hide out in the dressing room of the church; merely being alone with my thoughts will be enough.

There is no detail left undone. The sanctuary is beautiful, from the natural lighting that glows on the marble, to the antique candelabras at each corner of the aisles. Even with all the beauty that surrounds me, I can't seem to shake the thoughts that have been plaguing me since my return home.

Henry is sick. It's a fact I'm going to have to accept and deal with. There's a very real possibility that no matter how hard we fight this, he isn't going to win. Every time the dark thoughts loom, my stomach begins to ache, and it isn't just because of the fear. Something much worse is haunting me. Guilt.

Guilt ravages my thoughts. The times Christian and I had recently kissed replay over and over in my mind. The fact that I had been returning home to break Henry's heart, it is becoming a burden I'm finding hard to carry. On multiple occasions I've considered sharing my transgressions with Henry, but I know him too well.

He already tried to provide me with a possible exit from our relationship. If he finds out about my regrettable mistakes with Christian, he will assume I'm marrying him out of pity and never allow the ceremony to happen. I can't tell him.

In the past few days I've managed to distract myself with wedding details. Grandmother Wallace wanted to ensure all of the reception details were to my liking. Henry had always been a fan of their vacations in the Hamptons as a boy, so she wanted to bring the Hamptons to New York. I honestly could not have chosen anything better myself. As I see all the hard work she poured into the event I begin to regret the various control freak comments I'd made about the woman.

The menu is a traditional seaside lobster dinner, with long family-style seating, a request made by Henry. Even thought the guest list is quite extensive, he wants to do everything in his power to make it feel like an intimate celebration. The centerpieces contain touches of navy, white, and the gray from my bridesmaids dresses. She nailed the nautical details without it feeling like a cheesy, themed event.

Off to one side of the massive hall is a rustic rowboat

with *Henry and Paige* painted along the side. For the evening's events it will be loaded with ice and champagne. Staring at my reflection in the mirror before me, I can't help wishing that the ceremony was over and Henry and I were on our way to the reception. I have this uneasy feeling that something is going to go wrong. That somehow I'm going to—

"Paige?" My breath catches in my throat when I hear the voice behind me. I squeeze my eyes shut for a moment, hoping it's only my imagination. Then I hear it again. "Paige, it's me. It's Christian."

What is he doing here? My heart is racing. Opening my eyes, I turn my head slowly and see him standing at the entrance of the dressing room. The look on his face is one of sadness, which I don't think I've seen on him since his parents died.

I stand and turn to face him, a rush of panicked thoughts race through my mind. *What if someone sees him? What if Henry sees him? How do I make him leave? Is this my dream from months ago coming true?*

He doesn't say a word. He just looks at me, as if he's expecting me to explain myself. But there is nothing to explain. I already told him everything when I called. It was the day after Henry told me about the cancer. I'd had an entire night for the information to sink in, to understand what I was doing. I was even more confident in my choice. I wanted to be with Henry, to see him through the tough fight he had ahead of him. I knew if Christian found out about Henry's illness, he would assume I'd made my choice out of some false sense of loyalty and reveal my slip-up in Texas to Henry.

Instead I told him a variation of the truth, leaving out the bit about Henry being sick. I explained that once I saw Henry and our home, I'd realized that I'd made a mistake. I told him how I loved Henry and wanted nothing more than to be his wife, and I was positive what had happened between us had been an error in judgment.

He tried to argue with me, but each time I interrupted him sharply, ensuring him there was no use. I ended the conversation with a very direct instruction. I told him if he cared about me in any way that he needed to let me be happy, and to please never contact me again. Perhaps he would have still tried to plead his case, but I didn't give him the chance. I simply hung up, and prayed he would stay in my past.

But here he is now, staring at me. I widen my eyes, then in an irritated tone ask, "What are you doing here?"

He ignores my question and instead says, "My God, you look incredible."

"You can't be here," I snap. I can't let his compliments and charm affect me. It's a weakness I have, and I won't allow myself to betray Henry any more than I already have.

He moves closer to me. The room suddenly feels very tiny. Lifting his hands, he says, "You won't answer my calls, so what was I supposed to do?"

"Exactly what I asked you to do," I answer without hesitation. "I love Henry. You need to leave us alone. Let us be happy."

He flinches, as though my words cause him physical pain, and then shakes his head no. "I don't believe you."

"It doesn't matter what you believe." In the movies

ONLY IN DREAMS

such a gesture comes across as romantic and grand, but all I can think about is how selfish he is to come here. I shudder as the thought of Henry finding out what I've done pops into my mind. "I'm marrying Henry, and that's the end of it."

He moves closer, as I take another step back and now find myself against the wall. "No, something happened. It had to. You can't change your mind that fast. Did he say something to you? Paige ..." Christian pauses as he considers his next words carefully. "Did he threaten you somehow?"

I laugh. "Really? You know nothing about me, do you? You think I would be with someone so cruel? I made a mistake in Texas. I'm just grateful it was only a kiss and nothing else happened."

"It wasn't just a kiss, and you know that," he insists, before looking down at the ground, obviously struggling to hear the truth. My anger at his selfishness shifts into one of sorrow. No matter who is in my life, it seems I find a way to hurt them. I do love Christian. He was my first real love, and I know he'll always have a place in my heart because of that. How can I explain to him that a man who has done nothing but honor and support me for four years needs me, and that I love Henry enough to make it work?

It's clear to me he isn't going to go easily, and as much as I want to let him down gently, I need to get him out of here and fast. I decide it's time I pull out the big guns, so leaning forward I ask, "Just who do you think you are? You come in here and tell me everything I feel for Henry is a lie? Damn it, Christian! You don't know me anymore.

If you did, you wouldn't be here. Yeah, we kissed, it was nice, but that was it. It was the memories of what we were, but nothing we can ever be."

"Bullshit!" he snaps. "I know you felt it, too. That night I held you was the best I've slept in years."

Narrowing my stare, I look directly in his eyes. Forcefully, I say, "I'm sorry that moment was something more for you than it was for me. All it took was seeing Henry for me to realize my life is here with him. I'm not the same girl you fell in love with, and I think that's who you see when you look at me. I've grown into a strong woman, one too strong to just to fall back into a broken relationship."

"What are you talking about? I want you because you are strong. I see you for exactly who you've become—at least I thought I did."

"If you did, then you would know I'm exactly where I want to be," I reply softly.

Christian doesn't answer; he looks at me, his eyes watery. "Paige—" his voice cracks.

"I'm done talking about this. And I'm done with you."

"How can you be so cold? Are you trying to get back at me for hurting you all those years ago?"

"If you think I'm that petty, why would you even want to be with me?"

"I don't think—" he starts, quickly wiping away a single tear that escaped down his cheek. I force myself to think about all the pain and hurt he has caused me, all the things that would make me angry, so that I don't cry as well. I can't let him see me cry.

"You're the type of person who will always break

promises, and I'm not about to allow my heart to be broken again. That's why I need someone like Henry. He'll never hurt me."

He sighs. "So you want to be with him because he's safe, not because you love him?"

I cross my arms, guarding myself, and then answer confidently, "Nothing is safe about giving yourself to another person forever. The fact that you can even stand there and say that shows how little you know about real love."

"Enlighten me then." He no longer sounds hurt. Instead, his frustration shows through.

"When I imagine life without Henry, it's like imagining a world without oxygen." I hear voices outside in the hallway; this needs to end immediately, before someone catches a glimpse of Christian and gets the wrong idea. "You need to leave. Now!"

My tone surprises him. He looks me in my eyes and says, "I guess it's true. A guy like me only gets the girl in his dreams."

When he walks out the door I turn and collapse into a chair, clutching the tattoo on my wrist. *I just might take the chance.* Weezer's "Only In Dreams," begins to play in my head as if on repeat. I grab the towel on the back of the chair next to me and press it to my face, comforting myself. *It's over, don't cry for him, it's finally over. He has to hate you after that.*

~

CHAPTER 25

THE GUESTS ARE seated, the music is playing, my dress is gathered and draped in all the right ways, and most importantly, Christian is nowhere to be found. Scooping up my bouquet of flowers, I make my way through the door where Emmie is beckoning me.

"You ready?" she asks me.

I nod and smile as she takes my arm and leads me over to Colin, who is waiting near the entrance of the sanctuary. Suddenly, I am struck with a terrible case of deja vu, my dream still haunting me from months ago.

I look into Colin's eyes, then wish I hadn't. I can tell he's not happy, but I don't expect him to be. I'm sure if he had his choice, I would be marrying his brother. But it's not his choice, it's mine, and I am confident this is exactly where I should be.

Colin feigns a smile. I know he won't say anything to upset me, not this close to me walking down the aisle. Giving Emmie a hug, I reach out and take Colin's arm, and we both watch as Emmie steps through the doors.

Colin looks down at me. "You look beautiful," he says softly.

"Thank you," I mutter.

"Paige," he hesitates. I peer up at him.

"What is it?"

"Are you sure about this?"

I smile, press up on my tiptoes, and kissing Colin's cheek, I say, "More than anything." He doesn't know about Henry, and he can't know. I know he won't be able to keep it a secret from Christian.

He doesn't say anything else, only nods, and as the doors open the rest of the way, revealing us to the crowd that is waiting, we begin walking down the aisle, the guests rising to their feet.

I'm only a few steps down the ivory runner when I see Henry. He is standing at the end waiting for me. The moment his eyes connect with mine, I see an expression on his face that tells me I'm his perfect match and he's mine.

Our eyes never shift from one another, I don't see our guests, or notice the faces of my friends. It's Henry and I, here in this moment, together. When we reach the end of the path and Colin hands me off to my soon-to-be-husband, I realize how intense my smile is. My face is hurting.

I watch his eyes shimmer, revealing the emotion flooding over him. It's touching how moving this is for him, and I feel a flutter in my chest. My arm links with his as we turn and face the minister, who first greets the guests, then moves right into the ceremony. He speaks of timeless love and an unbroken circle. I try my best to concentrate on his words, but all I can think about is that I'm about to be Mrs. Henry Wallace.

Though I'm lost in the moment, the memory of that dream from months ago nags my thoughts. I swallow hard as the minister approaches the portion of the ceremony where he asks if anyone has any objections. Closing my eyes, I hold my breath and I wait. Each ticking second feels like an eternity.

And then it happens—the announcement is made, and it is official, Henry and I are husband and wife. I open my eyes wide, greeted by his smile. He leans in, first kissing me slowly, and softly, then suddenly without warning he grips my back, and dips me down low, pressing his lips firmly against mine. The crowd erupts with laughter and applause.

As he shifts me upright, I laugh, trying to make sure my appearance is not as disheveled as I feel. I'm pleasantly surprised by the sudden burst of energy and strength. "I love you." He mouths the words over the noise of the crowd. I smile, gripping his hand with mine and pull it up to my mouth, planting a kiss on his fingertips.

Here we go, I think as we make our way down the aisle, so much uncertainty awaiting us.

CHAPTER 26

$\mathcal{W}$HEN WE ORIGINALLY planned our honeymoon we'd dreamt of taking weeks off to travel around the world together. It was supposed to be a time for us to celebrate our marriage, focus on one another, and enjoy the newfound intimacy and security of being a married couple. The cancer changed our plans. Plane tickets were exchanged, and we shortened our trip to a quick five days up to Henry's family home in the Hamptons.

The doctors want to get him in for chemotherapy treatments as soon as possible, which means by next Friday we need to be back in New York, prepared to fight the battle of our lives. Even though Henry continually apologizes for the inconvenience, I actually am enjoying the last minute change in venue. Long walks on the beach, the sound of the ocean through our open windows at night, the cool breeze as it rolls in off the icy water. For him, these surroundings have always been a normal part of his life, but I rarely saw places like their summer home.

I open my eyes, deciding I had lain around in bed, pretending to be asleep, long enough. Much to my surprise, Henry is leaning over me, watching. "Good morning beautiful," he sighs.

"What are you doing?" I ask, shoving him gently, a little startled.

"I'm waiting patiently so I can greet my wife with a kiss on our first morning as a married couple," he tells me before delivering a devilish grin.

"Why Mr. Wallace, are you trying to put the moves on me?"

"Most certainly, Mrs. Wallace, is it working?"

"I don't know, keep trying, and we'll see." I smile.

Henry laughs softly, leans in close, and grazes my lips with his. The previous night's lovemaking flashes through my mind. Though Henry now tires much easier, his skills in the bedroom have not diminished with his illness. I couldn't have imagined a more perfect wedding night, other than a groom who isn't suffering from a brain tumor.

A brain tumor. My husband has a brain tumor. Even though I'd thought about it all the way to the house last night, I refuse to share my anxieties with Henry. There seems to be a lot of things I don't speak to Henry about these days. I keep telling myself that when he's well, I will be able to share more with him. However, right now, the last thing he needs is more stress.

Yet, no matter how many times I tell myself the secrecy is for his benefit, I am plagued by guilt. Like what happened between Christian and me. Telling him about what went on in Texas, or even that Christian tried to break up the wedding, will only serve to upset him, which is the last thing I want to do right now.

"Hello? Earth to Paige?" I hear Henry's voice break through my thoughts.

"Huh?"

"What's going on with you?"

I look at him, puzzled. "I don't know what you mean."

"I delivered you a pretty damn good kiss, if I do say so myself. I've been nibbling at your neck in such a way I doubt I could even resist myself, and you're just staring off into space. What are you thinking about in there?"

"I'm sorry," I begin. "I guess I'm still waking up. Here, try some more, let's see if you can get my attention." I shove his head back against the line of my throat.

He convulses slightly with laughter. I feel his hot breath against my neck, sending a chill through my body. "Oh yeah, how's this?" he asks, and then with wet, full lips begins pressing against my skin, tickling at my flesh and sending shivers down my spine. I arch my back in delight.

"Henry," I whisper softly, pushing into the motion with which his body is now moving. I can feel the anticipation increasing between my legs.

Suddenly there's a booming knock. Pulling away, I clutch the sheets to cover my bare breasts. "Is that someone at the door?"

Henry thinks about the question for a moment, and then bowing his head, moans, "Damn it, the chef."

"What? Who?"

"I hired a chef to come prepare an incredible brunch for us," he explains.

"Can you tell them to go away?" I ask, frustrated.

"I think that would be rude, don't you?"

"As rude as not keeping your new wife sexually satisfied on her honeymoon?"

"Oh—now you're just playing dirty. You stay here. I'll let her in so she can get started, and I'll be back in bed before you know it." Henry explains.

I furrow my brow, confused by what he is suggesting. "You want to have sex while that poor girl is in there cooking for us?"

"Great plan, right?" He smirks. "By the time we get done, we'll both be famished.

"Are you crazy?" I gasp. "Go let her in. We'll wait and eat like civilized people, and then it's back to bed."

He grins at me. "You're such a cock tease."

"Is that right?" I laugh, sitting up and slipping on my robe.

Henry jumps into a pair of sweats, then over his shoulder confirms, "Yes, yes it is."

"Mrs. Wallace, I'm going to ravage," he promises and then is out of the room, off to answer the door. I feel a tingle spread through my lower half. He has probably called me Mrs. Wallace a couple dozen times since we exchanged our vows, and I can't hear it enough. It literally makes my toes curl and my knees weak when he says it.

CHAPTER 27

*H*ENRY AND I have been having such a fantastic time on our honeymoon, I find myself forgetting just how sick he is. He's no longer the man I left in New York when I headed to Texas. Often, the slightest thing, like an icy breeze picking up off the water, can cause his chest and bones to ache. Though he tries his best not to complain, I can see the pain on his face.

It feels like we just got here yesterday, but it's already time to return to the city. I can see how much Henry loves it here, and I'd give anything to figure out a way to stay. To shut out New York, the doctors, and hospital visits, and stay here, in this moment together. The real world brings with it reminders of my mistake with Christian and of Henry's sickness. At least here I'm able to pretend that life is perfect.

I zip up the last bag and make my way into the main living area. Henry is napping in an oversized leather chair in the corner, the fireplace flickers and pops in front of him. I cross the room and sit on the arm of the chair next to him, staring into the orange dancing flames.

Without warning, I feel his arms wrap around my waist and pull me onto the chair with him. I grab onto the edge, trying to steady myself, and prevent the full force of my body weight from resting on his slender frame.

"I've got you," he says reassuringly.

"I don't want to hurt you," I explain.

"I said I've got you." With a deep breath, I release my grip and fall back onto his lap.

"I thought you were sleeping," I say.

"That was my plan."

"Is that right? You pretended to be asleep on the off-chance I would come over here and sit next to you?"

Henry snickers. "No, I pretended to be asleep so you would pack all the bags."

"Henry!" I exclaim, a huge smile spreading across my face. He pulls me in, close against his body, and kisses my neck. I sigh as the warmth of the fire surrounds us both. The moment couldn't be any more perfect.

"I love you," he whispers softly.

Pulling away, I look into his eyes, and before I even think about it, I suggest, "Let's stay here."

"What?" he asks obviously surprised.

I surprise even myself with the statement. Though I had the thought earlier, it never crossed my mind we could actually stay. But here, in this moment, I see no reason why we can't. "What if we stayed? I mean, I know Manhattan is our home, and I'm not saying we would never go back, but this place it's—"

"Magical."

"You feel it, too."

"I thought you wanted me to go through with the treatment?" Henry asks, confused.

"I do," I quickly add. "But why can't you go through the chemotherapy at a facility here? And then once the tumor shrinks, and you're ready for surgery, we can head back to New York."

Henry thinks about my proposition for a moment. "I suppose I can call Dr. Abbott and ask his opinion."

"Yes, there, that sounds like a brilliant idea," I agree, and my heart begins to race with excitement and anticipation.

"Winter in the Hamptons is absolutely incredible," he continues, naming off all of the positives he can think about with this plan. "And I'll really get some quality rest here. We can also have that chef we've been using come in and cook for—"

"Hey, wait, slow down, I think I can cook a few meals for my husband," I interject.

"Oh … well, I mean, I guess, if you really want to."

I laugh, pushing my shoulder into his. "Oh, come on, I'm not that bad."

"No, but I wouldn't exactly call you that good of a cook either."

"Too bad, our vows said for better or worse, and I do believe the worse part includes enduring my terrible cooking," I inform him, smiling gleefully.

"All right, if I must," he relents in a humorous tone. A silence falls over us, lingering for a moment. "There's something else I want to talk about with you."

He sounds so serious all of the sudden, I feel a flash of anxiety fill my chest. "What is it?"

"I don't want you to get angry with me."

"What on Earth could I ever get angry with you about?" I ask, now nervous.

"I'm serious. I want you to hear me out," Henry urges.

I sit upright, shifting my weight back to the arm of the chair. "You're starting to scare me."

"I don't mean to scare you, but we need to talk."

"So talk," I reply pointedly.

Henry sighs; he looks to the fire as if he were searching the colors for the right words.

"What's going on?" I demand.

His gaze shifts back to mine, as he takes my hand into his. "Paige, I love you more than anything in this world. I can't imagine my life without you in it."

"I love you, too," I add hesitantly. "Is this a bad thing?"

"No, I know you love me, and that's why this is so important for me to say," he begins again. "I want you to know that I'm going to fight this the best I can, and I promise, I won't quit until I have nothing left in me."

"You're going to beat this, Henry. *We're* going to beat this."

"Please, just let me get through this. I love you, and I am so happy that I get to wake up every morning for the rest of my life to your beautiful smile and terrible cooking. I want nothing more than to sit next to you when we're old and gray, in our rocking chairs, and watch the waves crash against the shore. But no matter how hard I fight, there's still a strong chance I'm not going to make it through this."

"Don't say that!"

He sighs and squeezes my hand tighter. "One of the few things that makes me really sad is the thought of you being alone if I don't make it."

"Stop it! You're going to be fine."

"Paige, please, this is important to me. If something does happen to me, and I don't make it, I want you to promise me something."

"I don't want to talk about this," I insist, then start to stand up, trying to pull away.

Henry tightens his grip, pulling me into him. "You need to let me say this. I can't bear the thought of you never allowing yourself to love again. If something happens to me, I want you to be open to being happy again. Promise me."

"I can't," I say, shaking my head.

Henry huffs, and I can see he's tired.

"We haven't even been married for a week, and you're talking about me finding someone else. You do realize how messed up that is, don't you?"

"This entire situation is messed up. Should I wait until I'm sicker, until this conversation might be too hard for me to have? I know you, and I know how you'll be if things don't work out. You'll retreat into yourself, never opening up to anyone ever again."

"What happened to a positive attitude? You said the doctors told you that is important. It's like you've already given up," I argue.

"No, I haven't, and if you'll just promise me that you'll move on when I'm gone, then I won't have to think about it anymore, and I can refocus all my thoughts on more positive things."

"I don't want anyone else, that's why I married you."

"I get that, but you might not have that option, and the idea of you spending the rest of your life alone out of some sick loyalty to me, or because you're scared of getting hurt again, makes my heart literally ache." His voice is starting to crack, and I can see how much the conversation is taking a toll on him.

I look down at my hands, fidgeting with my fingers and twisting my wedding ring in circles. I don't want him to worry about me. I want him to put all of his energy into getting well. I glance up; his eyes are already watching me. I take a deep breath, and with a slight nod, I say, "I promise."

Henry pushes himself out of the chair, wrapping his arms around me, and my head presses against his chest. "Then let's call Dr. Abbott and see if I can get my treatments moved."

~

CHAPTER 28

I STARE AT the words in the letter, struggling with pinpointing exactly how they make me feel. *We were so excited to hear that Henry seems to be getting better. The two of you are always in my thoughts. As soon as Henry's feeling up to it, Colin and I would love to have you two come down for a visit. Colin keeps joking about the forever-long honeymoon you two seem to be on, but I swear, I haven't said anything about Henry's condition, though I hope you will soon.*

I've now been Mrs. Henry Wallace for over two months. In that time I've taken my husband to more chemo appointments than I care to count and watched as his body shift into one I barely recognize. He has become lethargic, sleeping most of our days away. He's always nauseous and has wasted away even more over time, his body appearing bruised, as if it is being used as a punching bag. And if all of these things aren't bad enough, he also gets to deal with the loss of his hair. I've been by him through all of these things, careful to never come unraveled or project any of my concern onto him. But it does seem he is now finally showing improvement, and we have the opportunity to come out of our seclusion. It infuriates me that one thought continues to plague me —Christian.

I want to see Emmie and Colin more than anything, to spend time with Olivia, but going to Texas means I'll have to see him. I can't figure out if my concern is that he will reveal my indiscretions to Henry, or if it's simply the lingering guilt still haunts me. No matter the cause, the cloud is hanging over me, and even if we might be able to visit my Emmie eventually, I cannot think about that right now.

"Is that a letter?" I hear Henry's voice over my shoulder.

Quickly folding up the page and sliding it between the couch cushions, I turn and smile at him. "Oh yeah, it's just Emmie. Lots of Olivia stories, you know how she is. How are you feeling?"

"Actually," he says, pausing for a moment. "I feel great."

"Really?"

"Yeah, I mean it's hard to believe we're heading into the city already to see Dr. Abbott."

I stand and walk over, slipping my arm around his slender body, his bulky sweater slightly masking the change in his appearance. "I have a really good feeling about this," I announce.

"Me too," he adds and then pulls me in close, placing a tender kiss on my forehead.

"I can't believe he wouldn't give you some hint as to how the brain scan came out," I complain, picking up the last suitcase at our feet, and carrying it to the front door.

"He's a doctor, that's how they're supposed to act. I think they just want to be able to explain all the big words in person." I laugh at his comment, then slip the keys off the entry table and into my hand.

"How about I drive?" Henry offers.

I look at him with raised eyebrows. "Yeah, I don't think so. You might be feeling much better, but you still can't sit in a car for more than ten minutes without falling asleep."

"Yes I can ... I can last at least fifteen minutes," he insists.

"Exactly, now get your cute little ass in the car so we're not late. We have a two hour drive ahead of us."

"You know, I find this bossy side of you very sexy," Henry remarks playfully, leaning over to give me a kiss as he walks by.

I take a deep breath, preparing to leave the life we've made here in the Hamptons and take in whatever news the doctors have for us. I know there is a very good chance in a matter of days Henry could be heading in for surgery, and while it's terrifying, I also know it's the best news we could possibly receive.

I watch Henry as he walks down to the car. Everything has seemed to change over the past couple months. His face is now so slender most people can tell something is wrong with him. He walks with an arched back, as though he's trying to curl into himself as he moves.

Sometimes I tiptoe down the beach just to get a good cry out, determined to never let Henry see me come unhinged. A good purge every week has seemed to do the trick. But here we are, about to find out the news that could be the salvation for both of us. I lock the front door then stop on the steps, taking in a deep breath and smelling salt in the air. *It's time, no more waiting.*

CHAPTER 29

*H*ENRY SCOOPS MY hand up into his, causing me to stop picking at my cuticles. It is a habit I've picked up in recent months from all of the long waits in doctors' offices. "Sorry," I mutter.

"Don't be nervous, everything's going to be fine," he reassures me. Henry always leaves me wondering where he gets his strength. Let someone cut me off in a parking lot, and I have no issues finding the courage to put the fear of God into them, but something like facing your own mortality, and I know I would be a complete basket case.

"I'm not nervous," I insist. "I just don't understand why they make you wait in a waiting room, only to bring you into the doctor's office and make you wait some more. I mean, isn't that the entire point of the waiting room."

"It hasn't been that long."

"You're too nice. It's not like we're waiting for our takeout order. We're waiting to find out about a fu—" The word trails off my lips as I hear the door open behind us.

"Henry, Paige, welcome. I hope I didn't keep you waiting too long," Dr. Abbott says as he crosses the room, pausing to shake our hands.

"No, of course not," I quickly say, causing a low volume snicker out of Henry. With a gentle elbow to his side, he huffs then falls silent.

"Great, so let's see here," the doctor, an older gentleman with salt and pepper hair, and thin-rimmed glasses, says as he examines the file in front of him. "So, how have you been feeling?"

"Great—" Henry begins before I quickly interrupt with my nervous ramblings.

"He's been better than great Dr. Abbott., I mean, there was a while there that he was really struggling, and I wasn't sure. He wasn't eating, and he barely ever got out of bed. But in the past week or two he has been back to his old self. We even went on a walk a couple days this week."

"Yeah, what she said," Henry jokes.

I feel my face grow hot. "I'm sorry, I'm just excited. I know it's going to be good news."

Dr. Abbott says nothing. He doesn't look up, as Henry and I joke back and forth. He simply keeps studying the file in front of him, his face scrunched into an almost-frown.

"So when can I go in for the surgery?" Henry asks, sensing my uneasiness.

Dr. Abbott flips to another page, huffing as he reads the notes. Hesitating a moment more, he finally says, "Actually, it doesn't look like we're going to be able to do the surgery, Henry." When the doctor says his name, I shudder. There is more in the way he says his name than in his entire statement.

"I don't understand," I interject, realizing Henry is going to remain silent.

"We knew this was a possibility when we decided to move ahead with the treatment," Dr. Abbott continues. I look over at Henry who is nodding his head yes. It feels like I'm in the *Twilight Zone*, everyone around me knowing what is going on except me.

"I'm sorry, what exactly was a possibility?" I question in a stern tone.

Dr. Abbott looks at me with a sympathetic stare, and shifting in his chair so he can more comfortably look me directly in my eyes, says, "The tumor hasn't reacted to the treatment; in fact, it has increased slightly in mass. There's nothing else we can do."

"Wait," I blurt out. "What do you mean? How can that be?"

"We were all aware this was a likely outcome with this aggressive of a cancer at this late stage. Honestly, we were very fortunate we didn't have any incidents of infection during the treatment," Dr. Abbott informs me as if the terminal prognosis of my husband is something I should simply accept and make the best of.

"I'm not understanding. Are you saying we should just be happy an infection didn't kill him?"

"No, I just meant—"

"Please stop!" I say with a raised voice. "Is there any way we can we try the surgery?"

"I'm sorry, it would kill him."

"Is there a chance? I mean, hell, according to you the

cancer is going to kill him for sure. If he has a chance with the surgery we should do it. Right?"

"Paige," Henry's voice is calm, and I feel his hand come to rest on my leg. "It's going to be okay."

My head snaps back as I stare at him in disbelief. "This is not okay. I'm not going to be all right with my husband dying."

"There's nothing they can do," he says, which makes me suddenly feel sick to my stomach.

"Now, we do have several grief counseling services available to you," the doctor begins. I stand and, without a word, I turn and walk out of the office, deciding I'm not going to sit here and discuss all the amazing things they have available to help me cope and deal with the death of my husband.

I'M NOT SURE how long I stand in the hallway, random nurses asking me if I'm okay or if they can get me something. I want to scream at the top of my lungs, 'No, leave me the hell alone unless you can create miracles.'

When Henry comes out we don't speak. I'm not sure he knows what to say to me. He's the one who has just been delivered the news that he's going to die; yet he has to worry about me coming unglued. It's not until we make it all the way back to the apartment that I decide I'm calm enough to apologize for walking out.

The apartment is bright and airy, all of the curtains

have been opened and everything cleaned to perfection for our return. I approach the window, just in time to watch a few snowflakes fall through the air.

"It's starting to snow," I say, dreading the talk I know we're about to have.

"Are we going to talk about what happened?" Henry asks, no interest in the weather.

I turn to face him; he's standing at the back of the couch, watching me. "I'm sorry," I say in an almost whisper.

"I don't want you to be sorry. I want to know you're going to be okay." His words make my eyes fill with tears.

"How can I say I'm going to be okay after hearing you're going to die?" I look at him, knowing before I ask the question there is no possible answer.

"I know it's not what we wanted to hear, but—"

"I don't want to lose you." My voice cracks as I interrupt. He immediately closes the gap between us, wrapping his arms around me. I crumple into him.

"I'm so sorry you have to go through this." He sighs, his chin pressing against the top of my head.

I laugh, trying to wipe away the snotty mixture that's now running out my nose. "You're the one who is sick, and you're apologizing. I don't get you sometimes."

"I know this isn't how you imagined wedded bliss."

"I feel like our lives are just starting. It's not fair."

"No, it's not," he confirms. "But it's what we've got." I follow as Henry leads me over to the couch. He sits down and then guides me into his embrace, pressing my head against his chest.

"What are we going to do?" I ask, hoping he has a solution to a problem of which, in my heart, I know there is none.

He sits quiet for a moment and then clearly announces, "We're going to stay just like this, as long as we can."

"On the couch?" I groan, pulling my sleeve up to my red nose and nestling my head deeper into Henry's chest. I hear a deep rattle inside him as he laughs at my remark.

"Well, for now," he explains. "But, I mean more living in the moment. We keep each other living for the moment. It's all we can do."

My breath grows shallow. I close my eyes, taking in his smell, soaking in every sense the moment has to offer.

CHAPTER 30

*T*hree Months Later ...

I WALK DOWN the dim hall, careful to be as silent as possible, so as not to disturb Henry. Pressing gently on our bedroom door there is a slight creak as it opens. I peer inside. His head is completely under the blankets, and I can hear him gently whimpering in his sleep. I want to go in and hold him, but I know this will only make it worse for him.

Suddenly, my cell phone begins vibrating in my side pocket. I pull the door closed and back away carefully and quietly. As I make my way into the living room, I glance at the face of my phone. It's Emmie. I haven't answered her last two calls, and I know she must be getting worried.

Reluctantly, I swipe my finger across the phone and lift it up to my ear, then flop down onto the couch. "Hello?"

"Paige?" I can already hear the concern in her voice.

"Hey, how's it going?" I ask, as if nothing is wrong.

"What?" Emmie grumbles. "Oh, we're fine, but I've been trying to call you for over a week now, and you're not picking up. Is everything all right there?"

I sigh, pressing my head back against the throw pillow behind me. "Yeah, I guess."

"How's Henry?" she asks; I'm sure she can sense my mood already.

I hesitate then answer, "He's sleeping."

"Is he still feeling good?" she prods.

"I don't know. I guess he's fine."

"Paige, what's going on?"

I exhale deeply. "I don't really want to just unload on you whenever you call."

"Well, that's too bad. That's what friends are for. My job is to be here for you while you're going through this," Emmie insists.

"I guess."

"No, no guessing. That's how it is. Now tell me, what's going on?"

"I think I'm just frustrated," I say heavily.

"About what?"

"When the chemo was over, it was like Henry woke up out of this daze. The medication Doctor Abbott gave him to manage his symptoms was incredible," I explain.

"Yeah," Emmie interjects. "You mentioned last time we spoke how great he's been eating."

"It's not just his appetite coming back. Every night he wanted to go out to a different restaurant or meet up with friends. If our friends were busy, he'd make new friends. It was nothing like the homebody I was used to," I continue.

"You have to understand, he's facing his own mortality, and that's going to change him."

"I suppose," I agree.

"So what's bothering you? His new lifestyle doesn't fit you?" Emmie inquires.

"Oh God no!" I exclaim. "He's gotten back to a healthy weight and has been so active that I actually managed to convince myself that he was going to be okay, at least for a while."

"Well, sweetheart," Emmie begins. "You don't know, maybe we'll be blessed, and he won't get really sick for a while."

"No, that's what I'm talking about," I explain. "For the past few months Henry and I have been completely focused on enjoying each other's company. He gave up his position at the firm, I've put any plans for my line on hold, and it's been nothing but a focus on spending time together."

"That's great, I don't see the problem."

"Things started to change two weeks ago," I answer.

"What do you mean, they started to change?" she asks.

I swallow hard; I can already feel the burning in my eyes. I hate talking about Henry and this nightmare disease he has. "A week ago Henry's pain began to exceed what his pain meds could alleviate. As the pain has been growing in intensity, I've watched him struggling. He moans in his sleep, and he has trouble even walking around the apartment."

"Can they give him more meds?"

"Doctor Abbott says it won't help," I continue. "In the past ten days I think he's had a total of about five meals."

"Oh, Paige." I hear the pity in my friend's voice.

"I know. He gets weaker every day, and Doctor Abbott warned me that if I can't get his eating under control, we may need to think about a feeding tube." My voice cracks. "I can't force my thirty year old husband to receive a feeding tube."

"Have you tried to find something that isn't so hard for him to eat?"

"I've tried everything."

"Soups?" she presses.

"Everything," I confirm.

"What's Doctor Abbott say to do?"

The recent conversation between Doctor Abbott and myself flashes through my mind; it had been quite chilling. "He wants me to work with a hospice company, to assist me as he gets worse."

"Wait, wasn't he fine two weeks ago? Isn't that a little aggressive?" Emmie cautions.

"I don't know. He has me flipping out. He told me it can happen very quickly now, and I need to be prepared."

"For what?"

"For it to get much worse."

"Maybe you should hire someone, Paige," Emmie suggests.

"No, not you, too."

"This is hard enough on you as his wife. Do you really want to become his nurse too?" she questions softly.

"If that's what he needs me to be," I answer honestly.

"Paige?" I hear Henry's voice moan from the bedroom.

"Crap!" I exclaim. "He's awake, gotta go, we'll talk later."

"Okay, I'll call and check on you tomorrow."

"Bye," I say before hanging up the phone, not waiting for her response. I hop to my feet and rush down the hall, sliding in my socks to a sudden stop at our bedroom door.

"Henry? Are you all right?" I ask, pushing open the door and making my way across the dark room.

"It's my head," he begins. By the time I reach his side I see that he's gripping his skull with both hands.

The rancid smell of vomit drifts up, gripping my nose, but before it completely registers, I feel my feet slip out from under me. Placing a hand down on the floor at my side, I realize I'm now sitting in a warm, soupy puddle of puke.

"Oh my God," I gasp.

"I can't see," Henry moans, not realizing I had just slipped on his vomit. Panic floods over him, as I push myself up onto my knees, ignoring the mess.

"Baby, it's okay," I say. "Doctor Abbott said there was a good chance you'd start having some trouble with your vision. Just stay calm, it will pass."

"Jesus, it feels like the room is spinning," he cries. "I think I'm going to be sick again."

I immediately snap into action, standing and pulling him up to his feet. With his vision troubles he is hesitant, but eventually trusts me. "Come on, sweetie, let's get you in a nice cool bath. Those always help with the headaches."

I hear him whimper as we move toward the master bath.

"Are you okay?" I ask, trying to look at his face, slightly

swollen from the increased dosage of steroids he is now on.

"I'm so sorry," he groans, his voice cracking.

"Henry, there's nothing to apologize for."

"I love you so much," he insists, as I set him on the edge of the tub, making sure he is secure before turning and switching on the water.

"I know you do, and I love you, too," I say with a smile. "Now let's get you out of these dirty clothes."

He grips my arm, looking up at me. It's obvious he can't focus. "I shouldn't have done this to you, and I'm sorry. You have to forgive me."

With all of my clothes on, I step into the deep tub. Henry never let's go of me, but silently tilts his head from side to side, trying to figure out what I am doing. After I immerse myself, I tug on one of his legs and then the other, guiding him and helping to lower him between my legs, his shirt now drenched and clinging to his body.

"What are you doing?" he mutters.

"Shh, shh, shh," I hush him. "Lay back."

He does as I instruct. I wrap one arm around his neck, resting it on his chest, and with the other I cup the water and gently comb it through his hair.

I sink lower into the water until my lips are touching the tip of his ear. In a breathy soft voice I begin to sing, "I've got a daisy on my toe, it's not real, it does not grow. It's just a tattoo of a flower, so I'll look cuter in the shower. It's on the second toe, of my left foot. A flowering stem that has no root."

I feel his body tremble slightly as he snickers. "You're so weird," he grumbles before laughing some more.

I ignore him, finishing my silly song; "I've got a daisy on my toe, my right foot loves, my left foot so."

I sit, holding Henry in my arms, the water now rising to his elbows. I think about the water washing away this nightmare, bringing my Henry back to me. I know this won't happen, but I still think about it. Hope for it. Shifting in the tub, I lift a foot and use my toes to turn off the water. I feel Henry laugh again.

"What's so funny?" I ask.

"Your story about Emmie having monkey toes—how she can pick up almost anything with them."

"What about it?" I question.

"Just love that I have a monkey toe girl, too," he says, and I watch as he closes his eyes, a deep exhale pushing out of his body.

"Are you feeling better?" I whisper.

"Yeah," he moans, not opening his eyes.

"I don't want to be anywhere else," I say softly. "I just want you to know that."

He nods; I can feel him drifting off to sleep in my arms. I decide to give him a few minutes before we get out. I rest my other arm around him and lean my head back, closing my eyes for a moment. I'm not one to pray, but here in this moment I find myself asking for just a little longer before this new stage becomes our norm.

～

CHAPTER 31

*T*wo *Months Later ...*

THE CURTAINS ARE closed. I am careful to make sure they overlap one another, not allowing any sunlight to sneak in between the folds. It seems like the only way this makes any sort of sense is when the place Henry and I had created together, as a home, is shrouded in darkness. I can hear Emmie's mother in the kitchen, busying herself cooking more food than I will ever be able to eat.

"Can I get you anything, sweetie?" Emmie asks behind me.

I shake my head no. It doesn't even feel right when I hear my voice. It's hard to explain, but when I talk, it's almost like I expect Henry to answer me. None of this new reality seems right. It feels like something I'm going to wake up from at any moment.

Henry's grandmother has taken care of the funeral details—where his body was to go—but all of the styling options are left to me. I wonder how people do this all the time. Choose a casket, a color for the fabric inside; do you want an image on the tombstone or just words? What music would you like at the funeral? Will there be any special words read at the service? I was his friend for four years and his wife for seven months. How can I possibly answer all of those questions? How could he leave me?

I watch as Emmie reaches up to open the curtains I'd so carefully pulled closed the day before.

"Leave them," I gasp desperately, reaching up with one hand. Emmie stops and turns to look at me. I know this is hard on her, too. I can see she wants to fix it—that's what Em does. She fixes everything. But you can't fix this. It's like the hole that Henry's mother warned me about. It's so deep your body aches, wanting to find something to fill it, and you know nothing ever will.

"Colin called this morning to let me know he and Olivia made it back okay," Emmie says as she walks to the chair next to me and sits down.

"That's good," I reply, staring at a picture on the coffee table of Henry and I on our honeymoon. He looks like my Henry, not the man I said goodbye to. I want to tell Emmie to leave, but I know she won't understand. It's hard to be around someone who has her person still, after you lost yours. I never knew I could feel anything except love for Emmie, but somewhere inside me, there lurks a scarier version … a version of me who hates her. I hate Colin, too. I hate anyone who has what I lost.

"He was a good man, Paige."

I turn my head, glaring at my friend. "Was there ever any questioning whether or not he was a good man?" I snap.

"No," Emmie quickly replies, trying to find the words to state what she meant. "That's not what I was saying."

"Then what were you trying to say?" I ask coolly.

Emmie bows her head, exhaling deeply. "Just that I know you'll miss him."

I shudder, my shoulders folding in as I pull my legs close to my body. "I'm sorry, I shouldn't have snapped." My voice cracks as the tears begin rolling down my cheeks once again. I've cried so much since Henry died, that most of the time, I don't even notice when it starts.

"Sweetheart, it's okay," Emmie says, reaching out and placing an open hand on my arm. "Nobody can understand what you're going through but you. You're twenty-seven years old, you shouldn't have to deal with this."

"I didn't know you could hurt this much." As I speak, the nasal sound consumes my voice. The pressure in my head clicking and popping as the congestion from the hours of sobbing shifts in my head. "I miss him so much."

Emmie doesn't speak; she falls to her knees, and like the perfect friend she is, pulls me into her embrace. I wish I hadn't had such terrible thoughts only moments ago. I can't hate her—I hate the pain. Emmie rocks me until I lose track of time, the tears now dry on my swollen cheeks.

"I don't think anyone can understand your pain. All we can do is be here for you."

"I wanted to be there for him," I say.

"You were," Emmie insists.

"I know he hung on so long because of me. He knew I wasn't ready. They told us it would be within weeks after the chemo. Dr. Abbott said it was nothing short of a miracle that he held on for five more months. Henry kept telling me he was going to give me an anniversary. He wanted me to have that."

"He loved you very much."

"I wish we could have had an anniversary, just one. It would have meant the world to him," I repeat softly.

"You were his whole world. All that mattered was that he had you in the end."

I exhale, my chest shaking as I do. "I never realized what people went through when someone they love dies like this. I thought I did. I watched Henry go through it with his mother, but it's so different when you're living it. Did you know they give you a list of things you need to watch for if they choose to pass away at home?"

"No, I didn't."

"It's surreal. Thinking back, it's like it wasn't even me going through it. I feel like I was watching someone else's life play out. When your husband is thirty years old you don't expect to be watching for the signs it could be the end. How messed up is that?"

"You're going to get through this. Come to Texas with me, at least for a little while," Emmie pleads.

Lifting my head, I smile. "I can't."

"Why not? We want you to, you're our family."

I look away; I don't want her to see the truth in my eyes. I can't go to Texas because Christian is there. I can't be near him. I can't possibly grieve for Henry with him around me day in and day out. But that's just the thing. I should have known Emmie would see right through me.

"Colin can tell him about Henry's passing. You don't even have to—" Emmie begins.

"No!" I shout, turning to look her in the eyes. "You have to swear you won't tell him!"

"I don't understand. He cares about you, too. He'll want to help you get through this," she argues.

"I said no! Christian might want to help me, but he won't be able to stop himself. Eventually he'll want us to try again."

"Is that so terrible? You two obviously loved each other."

"Henry's body is barely cold, and you want to talk about Christian and me?" I can't hide the contempt in my voice.

"I'm not saying you rush into his arms, but you're are still young, Paige. You're going to fall in love again."

"Not him," I insist. "I almost cheated on Henry with him. I won't do that to his memory."

"Fine, but he's going to find out about Henry eventually," Emmie says. "He's already been asking questions. He knows something's wrong."

"Umm—" I hear Em's mom's voice from the doorway. "You have a visitor, sweetheart."

I peer past her and see Christian standing behind her; he looks like he hasn't had much sleep. I can't speak. I open my mouth, but the words won't come. I tell myself I need to shout for him to leave, but still, no words.

Emmie stands up, crossing the room to join her mother. "We'll leave you two alone."

Before I know it, Christian is standing right in front of me, alone in the room with the door closed. He crumples a piece of paper he is holding in his hand. It's obvious, he is struggling just as much as me for what to say. "I'm so sorry," he softly offers at last.

Finally something clicks in my head—anger—and with that I am able to find the words that have been escaping me. "Damn your brother."

I watch as he furrows his brow. "He didn't tell me about Henry. Trust me, I was pretty pissed he didn't."

"Then who?" I demand.

Christian hesitates. He looks at the paper in his hand and then back to me. "It was Henry, he told me."

I shake my head. "You're not making any sense, what the hell are you talking about?"

Christian quickly moves forward, shoving the piece of paper into my hand, and when he nears, I can see his swollen, bloodshot eyes. It's obvious he's cried recently. My heart stops for a moment until he steps back.

"Just read it," he instructs me.

My hands are trembling; the room is so dark, lit only by a lamp on the other side. I have to hold the note close to my face to make out the words. Immediately I recognize the handwriting. It belongs to Henry.

Christian,

We haven't officially met, but I feel like I already know you from what Paige has told me. She's a very special lady, isn't she? She won my heart the moment I saw her. I've spent the last four years trying to show her just how much I love her, and I hope I've succeeded.

I wanted to write you this letter to let you know I love Paige so much, and I want her to be happy. As happy as she has made me. I'm not sure if you know, but I'm dying, and if I've sent this,

I may already be gone. I saw you and Paige on our wedding day. The way you argued so passionately for her heart, and the look in her eyes.

Perhaps it was selfish of me to marry her after seeing that look, after knowing she felt the same way about you. I didn't want to die alone, and I didn't want to give up the one person who made me happier than I had ever been.

But now that I'm gone, I want that for my Paige. I want to know that she is going to spend the rest of her life loving and being loved, not mourning me. She deserves that. Help her live her dreams, hold her hand when you're walking next to her, she loves that, and hold her when she cries. She won't make it easy on you; we both know that's not her.

Fight for her, she's worth it. She's yours now, so please be there for her, and help her find that joy again. That joy that she gave me every day until my last.

-Henry

My arms drop down to my side, as I clench the letter tightly in my fist. I can feel my chest tightening, my breaths growing shallow. My brain's not sure what part of the letter to process first. He saw Christian and I on our wedding day? My heart aches to the point where I wonder if it might physically crack. I push that thought aside, and question what Henry could have possibly been thinking. I'm not something he could just give away.

"He must have sent it just before the end," Christian says.

"I miss him." I don't know why those words leave my lips, but it's all I have in me.

"I know." I hear Christian's voice shake, heavy with the

emotion of the moment. "He must have loved you very much."

"I can't do this, Christian," I quickly add as he takes a step closer to me.

"You can't do what?"

"I can't flip a switch and just be happy with you. Everything without Henry feels wrong." My chest heaves as I fight back the rage of tears behind my eyes.

Christian laughs softly.

"That's funny?" I snap.

Christian shakes his head, closing the gap between us. "I don't expect things to feel normal anytime soon. And I don't think Henry expected you to flip a switch either. Whatever will or won't happen between us, I'm not worried about right now. All I want right now is to hold and comfort the girl I've known and loved since I was a kid."

He stares at me—waiting for any sign his embrace might be welcome. I bow my head, which he quickly takes as an invitation. He wraps his strong arms around me. The zipper of his sweatshirt presses into my cheek uncomfortably, but the massive warmth and strength of his embrace is so intense I don't dare push him away. I almost welcome pain inflicted from something other than my cracked-in-two heart.

Gripping the sleeve of his sweatshirt, I crumple into him, the wall coming down and the raw pain enveloping me. "It hurts so bad." I cough and heave, my words barely audible.

He pets my head, he doesn't let go, and I cry as he

speaks, "Please let me be here for you, Paige. Will you let me do that?"

I nod, unable to speak, the pain in my chest more than I can bear. I have never felt so utterly broken. I can't process Henry's letter, I can't process anything except that I hurt. I hurt, and I don't want to. The loss is so great my body actually aches. I fall to my knees, curling into a ball, and try to shut it all out.

Christian is there, he moves with me, holding me, rocking me through my sobs. My eyes are burning, and I wonder if breathing will always be this painful. I struggle to breathe, Christian's broad hand rubbing circles across my back, trying to calm me.

I close my eyes; the warmth of his body and his steady breathing lulls me into the sleep that has escaped me for days.

CHAPTER 32

ne Month Later ...

SOME DAYS I feel strong—almost like I might be able to get out of bed and walk down to the table for breakfast. But just before I slip my robe on each time, the sadness creeps in, and I settle for pulling the blankets back over my head.

Then there are the days that I feel like I am a frail and broken leaf, laying on the ground, waiting for the massive storm that is just over the horizon to come and blow me away. Since I spend most of my time here, in this bed, staring up at the ceiling, I also have taken up a new hobby. At least that's what I like to call it. I worry. That is my hobby.

I worry I'll forget what Henry looks like. I worry I'll forget his smell, or his laugh. I worry there's nothing after this life, and I won't get to see him again. I worry I will get cancer and die a painful and terrible death alone—like

WENDY OWENS

Henry. I worry my friends will tire of me and send me back to New York.

Emmie can tell this is a new state of broken for me, and though she tries every day, I fear I am now becoming a burden on her. I then worry that Henry felt like he was a burden to me.

"Paige?" I hear Christian's voice and a knock on the tiny green door. I don't answer. He enters anyway. He's used to me not answering. "Are you hungry?"

I still don't answer. I simply stare past him. This never seems to bother him. He sets the tray he is carrying down on the small trunk at the foot of the bed and makes his way over to me, picking up a pillow I've discarded to the floor. He places it behind me and gently nudges me into a sitting positing, propping the pillow up behind me.

"Emmie made oatmeal. It's got raisins and nuts, and I brought up a little jar of pure maple syrup for you in case you wanted it a little sweeter," he says. I watch him as he retrieves the tray. I don't understand why he is doing this; I want him to stop.

"I'm not hungry," I say at last.

"Well, you need to eat something," he insists, pulling up a wooden chair next to me and placing the tray on his lap.

"I said I'm not hungry." My voice is dripping with venom.

"Then I'll sit here until you are," he informs me.

"Why won't you just leave me alone?" I ask, glaring at him.

"Because I care about you; we all do," he explains.

I huff. Deep inside me, I want the fight. I want to

unleash all my hurt, anger, and fury onto him, but I simply don't have the strength to expel that much energy. Relenting, I scoop the bowl off the tray and shove a spoonful of oatmeal into my mouth.

"There you go," he commends me.

I study him as he watches me just as intensely. I've been so cruel to him since I came down to stay with Emmie. I can't figure out why he puts up with it. "Can I ask you a question?" I ask after swallowing.

"Anything," he answers with a half smile.

"I got married to someone else," I begin. "Why didn't you move on, start dating someone else?"

Christian thinks about my question for a long time. Finally, he furrows his brow and answers me, "The same reason I didn't date anyone the last time we were apart. Nobody was you."

I shake my head, shoving another bite of oatmeal into my mouth. "Are you trying to tell me you would have stayed single forever if Henry hadn't been sick?"

"I don't know—maybe. It's hard to say. Perhaps, eventually, I would have found someone else who I connected with in the same way, but I just don't think that happens very often ..." He pauses, leaning forward. "For some people, it doesn't even happen once."

His dark eyes grab my attention, and I force myself to look away. I don't want to look at him. I just want to miss Henry. *Why won't he leave?*

"Does it make you uneasy when I say things like that?" he asks.

My head snaps back as I stare at him through squinted eyes. "No! Why would that bother me?"

"I don't know. It seemed to upset you."

"I'm not upset," I insist.

"Sorry, my mistake." I don't like the way he won't argue with me. Nobody will argue with me. It's like they all think I will lose all touch with reality if they push back.

"Do you come up here every day because you think eventually I'll give us a second chance?" I ask pointedly. I can see the question annoys him.

"I come up here every day because I care about you, and I don't want you to be alone with your pain."

"So you have no hopes of me ever loving you again?" I demand.

Christian shakes his head. "I can't imagine what you're going through."

"Answer me, damn it!" I shout.

"Pain makes us angry sometimes, and I'll be here for as long as you need someone to take it out on."

"Whatever," I huff.

Christian reaches out and grabs my hand. He pulls me closer, and I am suddenly uncomfortable. "Paige, I'll be here for you, but you'll never get me to stop loving you, so stop trying."

I feel my chest tighten, and my eyes fill up with tears. I wildly yank my wrists away. An awkward silence settles over the room. I wait for him to say something, to leave, to do anything, but he doesn't. He just sits in that damn chair and watches me.

I look to him, my voice shaking, and I ask, "What if I am never ready to be loved again."

"I'm not worried about that. I'm not even thinking about that," Christian answers softly.

"Because I may never be able to be with someone ever again. Do you understand that?"

He smiles, that crooked smile with his dimple, which is still amazingly sexy, but can't seem to pull me out of my stupor. "What happened to you is something you should have never had to go through, but you did. So right now, all I'm asking is that you take it one day at a time and let me be your friend. I'm not thinking about our future, or us, I promise. Will you let me be your friend?"

I feel my chest ache and tighten. I think about Henry's letter and what it must have taken for him to write such things to Christian. I feel so confused, and I don't know what to do, but a friend like Christian sounds amazing. I nod, no words seeming appropriate.

He reaches out and takes my hand into his. "What do you say to going downstairs and seeing Olivia and Colin and Emmie for a little bit?"

"I don't know," I say, hesitating at the idea of leaving the safety of my tiny room.

"How about you come down and try, and if you want to come back up, just tap my arm, and I'll come up with some excuse and whisk you back to bed," he offers. "Sound like a plan?"

"Okay," I agree and stand, wrapping my oversized robe around my small frame.

He opens the door, and as I step up to the doorway, I freeze, taking a deep breath.

"You all right?"

"I'm scared."

"I'm right here, one step at a time. I've got you, okay?" he encourages me.

I look at him then back at the hallway. On the other side of that door is the real world, the place where I watched my husband die. I can't believe there is a world where I am now alone, only looking out for me again. I glance back at Christian, feeling a chill run down my spine.

In that second I realize, I'm not alone; if I let them, I have my friends all around me, helping me one day at a time.

~

EPILOGUE

Three Years Later...

PULLING OUT ONE of the cardboard boxes from underneath the counter, I carefully lift and place it on the counter top, running the knife down the row of packing tape. I haven't seen my designs since I sent the revisions from the prototype off to the manufacturer. Taking a deep breath, I swallow hard and prepare to open the box, hoping this time they got it right. There is no more time for do-overs. There is just enough time to get the bulk order back before for the grand opening.

Opening one side of the box, and then the other, I peek through squinted eyes. I don't see anything too alarming at first glance—no clown costumes mistakenly packaged inside. Pressing my eyes wide open, I first run my hands along the pieces of clothing, taking in the textures. Pulling out the brown pants, I lift the corduroy to my nose and, with a deep inhale, smell. I'm surrounded by newness, and it's intoxicating.

Holding the pants out in front of me, I inspect the small plaid patches on the knee and the sliver just above the pockets, smiling at the perfection, pleased I'd made the choice to change things up at the last minute. Next, I pull out the faded denim button-up shirt, the beauty of it in the simplicity. Then at the bottom I see the piece that brings the outfit all together. It is the most delicious cream-colored, lush alpaca-haired vest. The medium-colored cowboy boots that came in the week before are a perfect complement.

Pushing the box to the side, I lift up the next, a small pink ribbon on the front of the label. The excitement in me is growing with each passing moment. I waste no time slicing into the box, my heart melting as I pull out the dress, masses of cream and soft pink tulle, billowing out from under the layers that are draped and cinched with the signature pink bow.

A bell chimes behind me as I hear the door open and close. I smile at the sound of Christian's voice. "Oh, I know you didn't lift those boxes up on your own, right?"

"Well, I looked around for some big, strong man to do it for me, but then realized we were in short supply of those around here and decided to do it myself."

"Ouch," he groans as he comes around the corner, clutching his chest as though my words wound him deeply.

"Aren't they beautiful?" I ask, staring at the newest pieces of the collection to arrive.

"They are, but certainly not the most beautiful thing in here," he says, lifting his chin and staring at me. It is that stare that, in my youth, made me uncomfortable, but the one that I now drink in with ease.

"Uh-huh, beautiful is about the furthest thing I feel right now," I say, pressing a balled up fist into my lower back.

Seeing my discomfort, Christian hops up and immediately takes action, leading me over to a nearby wooden chair and assisting me as I sit carefully. His hands run over my shoulders, and I moan as he begins to work the tension from my muscles.

"You know you shouldn't be working this hard," he comments.

"We open in a matter of days, so if I don't work this hard, we're not going to be ready."

"That's what I'm here for. You need to lean on me a little more," he insists.

"That's sweet, but you already built all of the furniture in this place by hand, and somehow managed to even find time to carve the clothing figures as well. I think you've done enough."

"We're a team, Mrs. Bennett," Christian says, and from his words I can sense his smile.

"Is that right? Well then, Mr. Bennett, I've been here all day stocking, where have you been?" I tease.

Christian lifts his hands, and I worry he may not realize I am just kidding. He walks around to the front of me, and lowering to one knee, he places a hand on my perfectly round belly and says, "I've been working on a surprise for the three of you."

"What?" I gasp, surprised by the news.

"Yup, and I think you're going to love it." Standing, he

extends a hand in my direction. I rise to my feet, arching my back to support the cumbersome weight of our unborn twins. When I'm finally upright I stare at him for a moment, his eyes so full of happiness that my heart aches. It's hard to explain, but when you were raised to feel like you deserve nothing in life, to have two men love you the way I have is quite overwhelming.

"All right lumberjack, where we headed?" Lumberjack is the name I've endearingly labeled my darling husband with. When we decided to open the clothing store in Bastrop, Christian declared he would not shave until opening day. I never realized just how sexy a full, bushy beard could be. I've come to love the way it tickles when he kisses my stomach, and now I don't want him to part with it.

"You'll see." He knows I hate surprises, which is why he insists on springing them on me constantly. I follow him out the front door, and it clangs shut behind me. Waddling down the wooden steps, I stare curiously at Christian when he stops only a few feet from the front of the shop. I look around us, but see nothing.

"Okay, I give up, what's the surprise?"

"Look up," he replies with a smile.

I turned toward the store, looking up over the display window and gasp as I take in the most beautiful piece of art I've ever seem carved onto a hunk of redwood. There, in big scrolling letters are the words **Henry and Ella's**, painted over with a soft blue and pink. Below that, in small script are the words Children's Boutique, painted in white. The background of the sign is the natural wood, and all along the edges are intricate engravings of leaves and vines.

"Christian!" I exclaim.

"Okay, hear me out. We knew we were going with my mother's name, Eleanor, for baby girl, but it seemed like we were having a hard time settling on a boy's name since Colin and Emmie named baby Thomas after Dad. I've been thinking a lot about it, and I wouldn't have you if it weren't for him. Hell, we wouldn't even have this shop; he found this building for you. It seems like it's only right we name our son after Henry."

My heart feels as though it might burst. I stand, staring at the sign, unable to speak.

"Okay, now I'm getting nervous, did I overstep? You hate it, don't you?"

I shake my head no, leaning forward and wrapping my arms around my husband's neck. "I think it's absolutely perfect."

"How'd she take it?" Colin shouts from the open gallery door across the street.

"She took it great!" I yell back, laughing.

Emmie emerges with Tommy in her arms and Olivia running out ahead of her. I watch as they cross, joining Christian and I in the street. This is it, here, all around me. This is what Henry meant. I was his family, and he wanted me to have the same thing after he was gone. He would always be a part of our lives.

Christian's lips touch mine, and my heart aches as he confirms this is real. I sigh as I think about my life, and how sometimes things don't always happen how we want them to or how we dream of them, but there is happiness out there for us if we're willing to let it in. Love like this, heart aching happiness—it's not only in dreams.

~

READ MAC'S STORY NOW

.

THE LUCKIEST

Married at eighteen, child at nineteen, widowed and alone at twenty-one, I've lived enough pain for ten lifetimes. - The Luckiest

When everything worth living for is suddenly taken from you, how do you keep going? People tell her how lucky she is just to be alive after that night, but she doesn't agree. The world doesn't stop just because Mac has lost everything, soon she will be forced to face demons she isn't yet ready to deal with.

PREVIEW OF THE LUCKIEST

I struggle to take a deep breath as the humidity overtakes my lungs; the pressure makes me feel as if I might drown. Squeezing my eyes shut, I try my best to block out all the sounds around me. The random coughs and whispering, the shuffling of shoes, rustling of papers, and in the rear of the room, the cries of a restless baby as the mother tries to comfort him.

There's no movement to the air in the old stone building, and I can't help wish to be anywhere else but here. There is a stench of sweat mixed with various perfumes hanging in the room, and I cover my mouth for fear I might be ill.

A hand settles on my arm. I know it's my friend Monica; she hasn't left my side all week. Her delicate skin on my flesh reminds me of a child—it reminds me of my Katie. I keep my eyes shut, steady my breath, and allow my thoughts to wander to Katie's smile, then her laugh. She's always had a joyous laugh, one that's fully committed. One that when someone hears it they can't help but smile.

I wonder if she is smiling now, wherever she is. Is she laughing? Is she making the people around her laugh and smile as well? I miss smiling. I wish she were here with me so I could remember what that felt like. I haven't smiled in so long.

My breathing is so shallow, I wonder if I might slip into unconsciousness at any moment. Does anyone around me notice I'm about to completely disappear from existence? I don't look—I can't. If I look, I know I'll see all the pity staring back at me. The eyes that tell me I'm alone now. The eyes that tell me I must have done something wrong, something that made my husband and daughter leave me alone in this miserable world.

As my heart begins to sink even lower, I'm consumed by the image of Travis's grin. He's waving to me. We're on the beach, and it's the summer right after our junior year in high school. His smile is so perfect. Suddenly, we're on the soccer field, and it's the day he first spoke to me, the day he changed my life forever. The day he took me from a wallflower, hidden from the world, and transformed me into a girl who everyone wanted to know, the girl who captured Travis Phillips's heart.

Does he still love me like he once did? He married me as soon as we graduated high school; he'd told me he couldn't be away from me another night. What changed? What did I do to make him leave me now? He can't have loved me as much as he said he did and leave me alone like this. I know Katie loves me.

Swallowing hard, I swipe the tear away that manages

to escape down my cheek. What if Katie is cold wherever she is? She needs her momma to tuck the blankets around her tiny body. My lips on her forehead each night are what push the good thoughts in, but who will do that? Who will read her a bedtime story?

I expel all the air from my lungs, and a calm settles over me as I remember she has Travis. He's such a good father. He will never leave her side. He will keep her warm. He'll read to her when I'm not there. He'll make sure the nightmares stay at bay when Momma can't kiss her goodnight.

"Mac? Are you ready?" I hear Monica's tiny voice whisper in my ear. I don't want to open my eyes. I know I need to, but when I do, time will begin to move again. I won't be able to stop it. This new world will become my reality. I will be alone. Once my eyes are open, everything that is wrong will sink in around me, pulling me into the darkness with its black tentacles, into the pits of tar that await to steal the last bit of life I have left inside me.

I feel Monica's forehead press against my cheek and her free hand cup the other side of my head, pressing me into her. The tender gesture sets off a reaction I can't seem to stop. I scream at myself within my own head to pull it together, but all composure is gone. My body starts to violently convulse, and I heave a breath of air in and out. A steady stream of tears follows the single tear that escaped only a moment ago, rushing from both of my eyes.

Monica grips me tighter and, turning into my crumpled frame, she begins to rock me. A whimper flees from my lips as she begins to pat my back. My father is a row behind me. I can feel his presence, but he doesn't reach out and touch me. He does nothing. He has done nothing to lessen my pain since I was twelve years old and my mother died. The cancer not only ate away at her body from the inside, but it didn't stop until it had consumed every last bit of the relationship between my father and me.

Somewhere in me, I know it hurts him to see me in such a state, but I don't have the energy to pretend everything is all right. If Monica were not here to hold me up, I know I would be in a ball on the floor—weeping and asking for mercy to end it. Daddy once told me it's better to feel pain than nothing at all, but I know now he was wrong. So wrong. A pain like this is worse than death.

When Mom died, it was like the wind was knocked out of me. What I feel today is so much worse. It's like the air has been stripped away, and I'm not even left with the desire to take in another breath. There's no fight for survival. There's no desire to see the sun set again. There's nothing but the pain and the hope it will end soon.

I hear the pastor's voice as a hush falls over the crowd. My back stiffens, and I manage to quiet myself for a moment. I need to hear every word. I know it will be like torture, but I have to. I'm here, and it's what I deserve for being here.

As if a switch shut off, the tears are gone, and I'm left with only damp cheeks and swollen eyes. Pushing myself upright, I inhale, the air shaking as it passes through my teeth. Monica's hand slides down and tightly grabs mine. I want her to release me. A desire to be completely isolated in this moment creeps in, but I don't pull away. I need to place my focus on what is about to happen, and I won't be able to do that without her supporting me.

"I want to thank everyone for coming out today. I'm sure I'm not the only one whose heart is breaking from this tragedy," the man standing at the front of the room begins.

I don't look at him. My nostrils flare in disgust; he doesn't know the first thing about a broken heart. I think he should be ashamed for even saying such a thing. His words string together into one meaningless token after another, until they fade into a dull murmur in my ears as my gaze falls onto the boxes only feet away from me.

Looking at them, it doesn't feel real. How can they be inside of them? They seem so small. They can't be comfortable, and even though I made sure the lining was soft and plush, I don't see how anyone could be comfortable inside. The outside of the casket is a pearl color. I have to fight the urge to stand and open the lids. The funeral home staff told me it would be best to keep them closed for the service. I understood why; they didn't look like themselves due to the impact of the accident. I was scared to say it at the time, but now I'm quite sure there could have been a mistake. If they don't look like themselves, then maybe it's because it's not them.

Though I'm trying to fight it, my mind wanders to that night. I wasn't conscious afterward. Maybe they took Travis and Katie to another hospital. Maybe they woke up and they're searching for me. I don't know who is in the boxes in front of me, but I can't believe it's them. I know if it were my Katie, I would feel it. I'd have to, wouldn't I?

The preacher my father hired is still talking. I try to

stand, but Monica's grip on me is too tight. I look at her, my brow narrowed. I want her to release me, why won't she...

She is looking directly at me. She shakes her head no, and her eyes are glistening. I clutch my chest. I can't breathe. The room is spinning. I want to pretend—why can't she just let me pretend? Maybe she sees it too. I don't deserve to pretend. I lived and they did not. I need to feel every second of life as I know it ending. The entire room sees it. They see that my innocent daughter was robbed of her life while I'm still here, still breathing, in and out. I want to tell them all that I wish I could take her place. Or even more, I wish I could take Travis's place. I'm jealous of him. Jealous that he gets to be the one to take care of her forever. He was always the strong one; he should be here, not me.

I'm smiling now, but I don't understand why. Perhaps out of fear that if I don't I may slip into an eternal madness. Married at eighteen, mother at nineteen, widowed and alone at twenty-one, I've lived enough pain for ten lifetimes. The smile slips from my face, and I'm again reduced to tears. Roller coasters of random emotions render me into a trembling mess. And in this moment I know there was no mistake. I'm alone. Alone on the brink of madness, left with only my dreams of once again holding them in my arms.

～

ACKNOWLEDGMENTS

FIRST, THANK YOU to my readers. Without you, what I do would have no purpose.

To my Sister Tammy. I dedicated this book to you because much of the inspiration behind Henry came from Mark. We all miss him every day but I can't begin to imagine your pain as his wife. I hope you find peace in knowing he waits for you in eternity and I equally pray you are able to find love again her on Earth. Mark loved you so much he would have wanted you to be happy, of that I am certain.

Madison Seidler, your honest and tough feedback helped me turn this book into something I'm very proud of. Thanks as well to Chelsea for polishing up the final product.

Sometimes being an indie author can make you feel like you're on an island. Thanks to ladies like Samantha Young, Ella James, Amy Miles, and the countless others who take the time to lend advice or sometimes just an ear.

To my husband, thank you doesn't seem like enough.

You work hard building your own business, but somehow always manage to find time to help me. Your support keeps me going, and I always know if I have a 2AM meltdown, you will be there to hold me together. You're a pretty darn good kisser too, so thanks for that.

For my three beautiful children, thank you for tolerating my schedule when deadlines are looming. Thank you for the unconditional love. And thank you for the endless inspiration you provide me with.

~

ABOUT THE AUTHOR

Wendy Owens was raised in the small college town of Oxford, Ohio. After attending Miami University, Wendy went on to a career in the visual arts. After several years of creating and selling her own artwork, she gave her first love, writing, a try.

Wendy now happily spends her days writing, though she still enjoys painting. When she's not writing, she can be found spending time with her tech geek husband and their three amazing kids.

For More Information:
www.wendyowensbooks.com
me@wendyowensbooks.com
ALSO BY WENDY OWENS

Find links to all of Wendy's Books at
wendyowensbooks.com/books/

PSYCHOLOGICAL THRILLER

My Husband's Fiancée (book 1)
My Wife's Secrets (book 2)

The Day We Died
An Influential Murder

Secrets At Meadow Lake

COZY MYSTERIES
Jack Be Nimble, Jack Be Dead
O Deadly Night
Roses Are Red, Violet is Dead

YA ROMANCE
Wash Me Away

CONTEMPORARY ROMANCE (adult)
Stubborn Love
Only In Dreams
The Luckiest
Do Anything
It Matters to Me

YA PARANORMAL (clean)
Sacred Bloodlines
Unhallowed Curse
The Shield Prophecy
The Lost Years
The Guardians Crown

Made in the USA

Made in the USA
Monee, IL
23 November 2023

47089453R10164